Mendell St

Mendell Station

A Novel

J. B. Hwang

BLOOMSBURY PUBLISHING
NEW YORK · LONDON · OXFORD · NEW DELHI · SYDNEY

BLOOMSBURY PUBLISHING
Bloomsbury Publishing Inc.
1359 Broadway, New York, NY 10018, USA
50 Bedford Square, London, WC1B 3DP, UK
Bloomsbury Publishing Ireland Limited, 29 Earlsfort Terrace,
Dublin 2, D02 AY28, Ireland

BLOOMSBURY, BLOOMSBURY PUBLISHING, and the Diana
logo are trademarks of Bloomsbury Publishing Plc

First published in the United States 2025

ISBN: HB: 978-1-63973-618-8; EBOOK: 978-1-63973-619-5

LIBRARY OF CONGRESS CATALOGING-IN-PUBLICATION DATA IS AVAILABLE

2 4 6 8 10 9 7 5 3 1

Typeset by Westchester Publishing Services
Printed in the United States at Lakeside Book Company

To find out more about our authors and books visit
www.bloomsbury.com
and sign up for our newsletters.

Bloomsbury books may be purchased for business or promotional use.
For information on bulk purchases please contact Macmillan Corporate
and Premium Sales Department at specialmarkets@macmillan.com.

For product safety-related questions contact productsafety@bloomsbury.com.

For Eunice

I

"Miriam, why do you want to work for the postal service?"

"I want a career change." I quoted the informational video they'd shown me ten minutes before the interview. It was hard to focus, but I registered an affinity for my interviewer. Her dark lip liner, shimmery eye shadow, and curls with a wet look from gel or mousse hinted at a combination of fun and no-nonsense.

I asked if it was true, like they'd said in the video, that I'd have to walk ten miles a day.

Rocio looked up from the form she was filling out, rapidly circling things without asking me any questions.

"It depends on which station you're sent to. But probably not. Or probably not every day."

"It's all right. I can do it. I was just curious." The last time I'd walked ten miles on a hike, years before, I was so out of shape I hadn't been able to stand up without support the next morning.

"One good thing about the postal service is you can start in one place and move around," Rocio said. "I started out when I was eighteen, a few years of mail handling in the processing plant here.

Then I moved into human resources, then sales, then back to HR. Just get your foot in the door. I mean, you could work for Google or Apple or whatever"—she rolled her eyes—"but I hear they have layoffs. The postal service hasn't laid anyone off since 1775."

This was the hot ace in her pocket. It worked on me, though likely not in the way Rocio intended. I smiled at her unexpected comparison to Google and Apple, which reflected the populist anti-tech sentiment in San Francisco.

"What part of town do you live in?" she asked.

"Parkside."

"They'll probably put you there, not move you around to some random station every day like they used to for new hires. They're really trying to keep people now."

I batted away questions about why the turnover rate was high. I lived a fifteen-minute walk from the Parkside Post Office in a foggy residential neighborhood by the beach. At thirty-three, my minimum living expenses (rent, utilities, groceries, car, dog) were $2,400 a month, which the $20/hour would cover. The government health insurance and retirement packages were better than at the private school, but the job paid about $20,000 a year less than teaching, and I'd be giving up my summer vacations. I didn't care. There was only one concern.

"So, 'part-time flex' means I'm not guaranteed forty hours a week?"

Rocio laughed. "PTFs are asked to work overtime every day, except a few weeks in the spring when it's slow—the only reason it's called part-time. Trust me, by then, you'll want a break."

The conversation was less an interview than an opportunity for Rocio to convince me to accept the inevitable offer.

* * *

My path to this interview had started three weeks prior when my best friend's roommate, Patty, a half-Asian waif butch dyke with elfin features and a quiet, electric intensity, texted me during my daily morning devotional. I was drinking Bustelo and left-over soup, and the Bible was opened to Ezekiel 4, the chapter where the prophet did crazy performance art. First, Ezekiel pretended a brick was Jerusalem and besieged it, then lay on one side for 390 days and on the other side for 40 days, to symbolize the years of punishment, while eating strange bread baked on cow dung. It was supposed to be human dung, but Ezekiel protested, and God acquiesced to cow. My favorite act was when he shaved all his hair and beard and weighed it, so he could burn a third, strike a third with a sword all over the city, and throw a third into the wind. I tried to imagine a biblical crowd watching the bald, clean-shaven prophet whacking at his hair with a sword, his face filled with dread and doom.

Then Patty, who did not have a habit of texting me at seven in the morning, sent a torrent of information: Esther hadn't come home the night before. She wasn't answering her phone. Her last texts were at two A.M. about wanting a late-night burger, then about going back to the bar where she'd left her credit card. Her backpack and shoes weren't home, no empty glasses in the sink, no sign she had been back.

Which bar? I texted back.

I don't know. She was out with Minyoung. Patty's girlfriend. Another of our friends, Minyoung was a K-town Korean transplant with what Esther affectionately called a "resting cunt face."

Esther went to her dance class last night, Patty texted.

Could you ask Minyoung what bar they went to? Then, *Never mind, I'll ask her myself.*

I thought of all the dangers facing a drunk woman alone late at night in the Tenderloin. When Minyoung didn't respond right away to my text, I called her.

I heard the fatigue in Minyoung's voice sloughing off. "We were at Nite Cap. Fuck. I should have walked her to Muni."

"All of us have walked drunk to Muni before. Let's just hope she's okay."

"Now that I think about it, she was pretty bad. I almost wondered if Esther was on something when she showed up to my dance class. Then she fell so hard at the bar that the bartender refused to serve her any more."

"That bad? Was she able to hold a conversation?"

"No, yeah. We talked."

On my drive to work, I called the middle school where Esther was their favorite substitute teacher. The school secretary confirmed Esther was scheduled that day but hadn't shown up. On my lunch break, I pounded on Patty and Esther's apartment door and waited, hoping Esther had drunkenly slunk in while Patty was at work. I taught my high school students with an unstable stomach, silently praying between every class for Esther's safety. Patty called the hospitals in the area, and Minyoung called the police stations, both asking if anyone had found her or an unidentified Asian American woman in her early thirties. During my conference period, I sped downtown to Nite Cap in the January rain. I remembered when a kind stranger had woken me up on the sidewalk after I'd had too much to drink, so I combed the streets for her passed-out body. I imagined Esther with blood and semen dripping down her legs from being raped and tossed in the back of an unmarked van. How could I ever face her if I didn't try everything to find her? After school, I banged violently on her apartment door again. I prayed to God that she wasn't opening the door because she had the worst hangover of her life. The sky began to darken, and Patty confirmed Esther hadn't come home, so we decided to file a missing person report.

I debated whether I should call Esther's parents or one of her brothers. I settled on her brother Charles, to whom she was closest. For some reason, instead of picturing him as the slightly balding, avuncular man he was, I remembered his gel-slicked hair and baggy jeans as a teenager, the annoyed but resigned way he drove Esther and me to Amoeba Records, Modest Mouse, and Sleater-Kinney concerts in L.A. The oldest, he was like a third parent, a bully, a confidant, and a protector. It took everything to steady my voice and tell him his younger sister had been missing since last night.

"Esther passed away," he replied.

"What?"

"Esther's dead. My parents got a call this morning from SFMTA."

The love I had for Esther distended and became a fluid that filled my skull.

In a slurred voice, Charles said Esther had fallen two stories onto the train tracks at Van Ness station.

My skeleton felt ripped out of my body, and I crumpled to the floor. The sound of many waters, weighted clouds in the sky, thin black grooves between the wooden floorboards teeming with darkness.

Charles asked for Minyoung's phone number. In slow motion, I pushed my attention to my phone. I watched myself from a distance scrolling through my contacts list, zooming in on each digit. The numbers were indecipherable, possibly in another language. On the other end, Charles kept asking me to repeat myself. We stuttered and echoed the same numbers back and forth. Most of the call was this demented exchange.

When we hung up, I instinctively dialed my mother. Hearing her voice made a childish cry burst from my mouth: *"Omma!"* At once I began weeping.

My mother was neither warm nor maternal, but the way I called out must have aroused uncharacteristic shock and concern. In Korean, she shouted, *"What is it? What happened?"*

"They say Esther is dead."

"What? What do you mean?" I could hear impatient murmuring from another woman in the background, probably a hair-dyeing customer. My mother must have been in her beauty salon.

"At the subway station, they say she fell two stories onto the tracks."

"Oh dear, oh dear. Oh Lord . . ."

I wept into her listening ear until I remembered Minyoung and Patty. The whole day we had been looking for Esther when she was already dead. I told my mother I'd call her back, and I texted the group the news. One by one, they called me, crying. Patty screamed.

Evening brought downpour and thunderstorm, and knowing we couldn't be alone, we met at my apartment with my anxious dog.

Esther had met all our families and remembered the names of every last cousin, aunt, and uncle. If any of us wore anything she liked, she called dibs on it in case we threw it away. Her famous lentil-salad recipe was from the café she worked at, but she also made a disgusting pot of lentil stew during a camping trip. She was obsessed with her childhood beagle, Maggie, whom she drew on any dusty car window she could find. Her extreme cheapness (she stole toilet paper from restaurant bathrooms) combined with her generosity (she once gave a stranger the socks off her feet). She washed dishes quickly but not thoroughly; she did not mince garlic finely. She preferred walking across the city to taking the bus, resulting in solitary treks, a deep tan, and an outside smell mixed with her essential oils. She had a capacious sense of time—she rarely was the one to end a hangout. She would never leave a friend hanging when the friend needed someone to go out with. She jumped in the icy ocean in the winter, bought hoop earrings from Michaels, held American Spirits loosely between her index and third finger. None of these things captured her. I was scared. Cannonballs had shot through an elaborate structure of toothpicks.

That night, I dreamt her rotting body tried to devour me. I let her teeth sink into my flesh because I loved her. In the morning, the double blow—she was dead, and it was real.

The first week, my vomit and diarrhea were physical signs that I was trying to expel the news from my body. I kept repeating to God that she needed more time, to please have mercy on her soul. I cried out to Esther in my mind, telling her to run toward the light instead of away from it. She had said Christianity sounded nice, but she couldn't quite believe it. Then prayers no longer came out of my heart.

After managing a few hours of sleep a night, I woke up every morning to the same mental image: a kitchen knife being slowly inserted into my temple. The loss had unlatched a door in my brain, unleashing my past experiences of human fragility—my chronically ill father, his death, my mentally ill mother, my suicidal days. My father had passed away after years of a wasting disease, and those years returned as a pounding ache, compounded by the blow of Esther's departure. Driving became dangerous because of my blurred vision, but I couldn't take the train because the sound of the rails undid me. From continuous eating—entire bags of chips, king-size bags of Snickers Minis and Twix, entire pots of soup meant to last for days—I gained ten pounds in a week before realizing that the hunger I was trying to satisfy was otherworldly.

I had been teaching Scripture at a private Christian high school, and my next unit happened to be on God's wrath. I had taught these lessons before, but it felt as if I were intruding on a stranger's documents.

- God's wrath = just, perfect (Romans 2:5)
- Righteous anger vs. sinful anger (Psalm 4:4)
- How does our wrath compare to God's? (Malachi 2:3)
- Objects of God's wrath:
  - Injustice: oppression, extortion, murder (Exodus 22:22–24, Joshua 7, John 2:14–17)
  - Jealousy: intermarriage (Numbers 25:1–9), idol worship (Exodus 32:10, Deuteronomy 28:15–68, Zephaniah 1)
  - Lack of faith: fear of Canaanites (Numbers 14), census (1 Chronicles 21)
  - Worshipping incorrectly: unauthorized incense (Leviticus 10:1–2), the Pharisees (Matthew 12:34)
  - Sin, everyone (Romans 1:18, Psalm 14:3, 53:3)
- Measuring God's wrath:
  - Every day (Psalms 7:11), but for a moment (Psalms 30:5)
  - Punishes 3–4 generations, blesses 1,000 generations (Exodus 20:5–6)
  - Slow to anger (Exodus 34:6), ready to forgive (1 John 1:9)

When I got to *How do we understand God's violence?*, I remembered what was there and couldn't look: the ground opening up and swallowing families, dogs licking Jezebel's bones, fire from heaven, leprosy, tumors, plagues, righteous mass stabbings, the smiting of every firstborn, angels of death, siege and exile, starved women eating their own afterbirth, and battle-armored locusts with human faces, women's hair, lions' teeth, and scorpion tails.

I remembered wanting to guide my students in a theology of suffering, as they reckoned with the violence in the Bible, an omnipotent God, and the pain in our world. I taught a mix of literal and literary explanations, but after Esther died, all I could think about was God's wrath pouring onto her soul. Her body was already mangled—to destroy her soul seemed sadistic. Esther didn't believe in God, and unremitting thoughts of her in hell tortured me. Instead of providing comfort, my faith drove me insane. I tried to reason: Esther falling to her death would have sounded absurd a few days ago, but it was real. What if her condemnation was as well? I questioned how crazy I was for ever believing this. Wasn't I an intelligent, thinking woman? But trying to remove hell from my Christianity revealed what an essential pillar it was. Hell touched everything. Salvation from it was the root of our praise, forgiveness, grace, evangelism, and charity.

I wondered if anything else I believed about my existence—my family of origin, my hometown, America, the solar system—was about to crumble. My brain was a computer with water poured on it. For the first time in my life, the tenet that God's natural inclination toward me was rage until He tortured His Son to death on the cross made Him sound like a maniac. I had left my abusive parent's home at eighteen, but if God was almighty, unlike my childhood home, I could never leave his domain.

After Esther's death, I only went to church that first Sunday. I haunted the coffee and snack table in the foyer, unable to enter the sanctuary. I wept at the familiar songs of praise and redemption, at the line of congregants in the aisles opening their hands and mouths to consume the blood and the body, broken for us.

Work was no better. For five class periods a day, I got up in front of my Scripture class with a blocked-up red nose and swollen-flesh pillows under my eyes, popped in a nature documentary, and sat outside on the cold linoleum tiles with my back to the wall. Weekly community groups at church met without me, and nobody complained when I canceled the dinners that I'd signed up to cook. Congregants offered to come pray with me or visit with food, and I politely declined.

Esther's absence haunted Patty's apartment, so Minyoung moved in with her. At an age when most of my peers were getting married, I, too, walked down an aisle between pews, toward my best friend in a white dress, in a casket. Someone had dolled her up in a gaudy corpse costume. Her parents or the mortician? Yet the reason I couldn't stop shaking as I walked toward her was verified when I saw her. The body was her, and it wasn't. Her square jawline, tanned skin, gangly body, voluminous hair. Her. Not her. Despite what ruins were left of my faith, the language of the sacred and profane felt appropriate. Death had defiled her divine, living form.

Patty and Minyoung sympathized with me but didn't fully understand my crisis. Neither of them was religious, though Minyoung was kind enough to find us a secular grief counselor named Dennis, who led group sessions at the Institute on Aging. At the first session, in a room full of older people with graying or white hair, Dennis asked the room what we'd been taught about death, how the adults around us had dealt with it. Most shared that death wasn't spoken of. Adults either refused to bring up lost ones or were afraid to do so. Dennis said Western culture was a death-denying society that ill-prepared us for the inevitable.

* * *

During my weekly check-in call with my mother, I admitted I hadn't been going to church. When she asked why, I told her I couldn't stop thinking about hell, and whether Christians really believed Esther, or anyone like her, was there.

"She was going to church with you, I thought." My mom had known Esther since she and I were teenagers.

"Yeah, but she didn't believe in God."

"How do you know?"

"She told me."

"Why do you keep thinking about hell?"

"I can't help it! I'm worried about Esther."

"Trust that God is good."

"Don't you believe God sends nonbelievers to hell? Is that good?"

Her voice turned sharp. *"The more you think about things you'll never know, the more you needlessly stress yourself out."*

I switched to English in anger. "If I died without believing in God, you would just not think about it?"

"It sounds like you've already decided to lose your faith."

"It's not a choice! You believe or you don't."

Some heard the gospel and believed it. Others didn't. Choice wasn't involved—it was intuition, in the guts. Visceral. My experience made me guess that the capacity for human beings to change their minds only appeared for short windows at a time and was often traumatic and involuntary. For people to have the ability to regularly change their mind about fundamental beliefs was either an enlightened state or a troubled and unstable one.

At the end of the week, a student stepped out into the hallway where I was sitting on the floor to inform me that they had now seen every episode of *Planet Earth*. I looked up at him and responded, "I'm not fit to teach." I assigned silent reading to the class while I wrote a resignation letter at my desk. That night, I prepared lesson plans for my replacement.

It helped to stop feeling pressure to form strings of sounds about God and to know those sounds wouldn't have to enter my ears. Only after I quit my job did my appetite, digestion, and sleep began to stabilize. But my body's return to normal when nothing was normal alienated me from my own flesh.

Other than the weekly grief groups at the Institute on Aging, I was stuck at home. I pictured Esther sitting on my floor cushion, doing yoga poses on my carpet, swinging on my kitchen stool, smoking cigarettes in my backyard. Every place I went in the city—even the grocery store, gas station, park, café—carried memories of Esther. I needed to leave the house, but I couldn't look at anything.

That was when I saw an Asian mailman in his sixties, swimming in his oversize uniform on the sidewalk. The warmth I felt toward the uniform surprised me. The baby-blue collared shirt with the small eagle flying over the breast pocket, smoky gray-blue slacks with a navy stripe down the length of the side, stylish metal chain for the keys, white plastic safari hat. There he was, standing under the shade of an awning, keenly studying a magazine he was supposed to deliver—also cute.

I remembered Esther walking alone through the city and how her favorite aunt was an artistic spinster and retired mail handler for the postal service. The aunt had refused treatment when diagnosed with cancer, and during Esther's visits, they smoked weed together to help with the aunt's pain. She had earned enough money over her lifetime to bequeath a house to Esther, not knowing Esther would join her so soon after. For a few months, Esther was a homeowner, a rare feat in our group of friends. When I'd asked what she would do with the money from renting out the house, she answered, "I want my parents to retire." From all her penny pinching, she'd save up a couple grand here and there to travel with friends. When she died, she had been planning to go to Mexico with a co-worker friend in February. She knew how to live.

I approached the mail carrier and asked if he liked his job. I asked what his hours were, what his typical day was like, if I should be a mailwoman. He smiled and replied with an answer I wanted to hear—not the words themselves but his meek resignation, dark humor, and protectiveness: "You're too young to waste your life doing this."

Then he asked, "Why you want to do this?"

"I want something physical. And I want to be alone."

*   *   *

I felt at ease among the cockeyed fixtures at the mail-processing plant. Before the interview, I had entered the building, passed through security, and seen an easel announcing the number of workplace accidents and the reduction goal. Despite the grim significance of the numbers, they were big and colorful. Above the easel a ratty banner hung over the double doors, emblazoned with LET YOUR SMILE CHANGE THE WORLD. DON'T LET THE WORLD CHANGE YOUR SMILE and a piece of Microsoft clip art: a yellow flower with wide eyes and a cheerily deranged face. The banner was like a smile with a bit of food stuck in its teeth, conveying effort and futility at the same time. The informational video was crooked, sliding off the screen. The processing plant evoked in me the feeling of politely trying not to notice a fart in an elevator, and I reflected on the customary pardon extended in such situations.

*   *   *

After the interview, I took my dog, a fawn-colored Jindo, out for a walk. Dolmangi, which in Korean means "small, smooth stone," was what my mom named him, before growing tired of having a dog and giving him to me.

We headed toward Ocean Beach when the world was dimming, and the setting sun lit up a hillside of dried, wild grass. The thin blades overflowed with light—fragile filaments with dissolving boundaries. They were on fire without burning, like Moses's bush. As the sun lowered toward the horizon, a breeze swept through the blades, causing them to tremble in unison. By accident of sun and wind, the dried husks became an ecstatic multitude bursting with light, as if involuntarily filled by the Holy Spirit. How helplessly the grass shook against its will! I was moved by this material display of resurrection. Looking down, I saw that the receding sun caused the edges of my own hand to glow. I felt insane. I couldn't shake the light off. If there was no hell, was there no heaven for my father, no hope of reuniting with him in a perfect future? I had always believed his spirit was eternal and next to God. But his posthumous existence was suddenly in question, as was Esther's.

When Dolmangi and I got back to our apartment, I realized I'd left without the keys again. The day before, I'd installed a lockbox with spare keys: a tacit admission that my mental state was not going to improve anytime soon.

I fried an egg and ate it with rice, kimchi, and sesame oil in the dark. It helped not to see all the emptiness.

2

The two-week orientation and training included short, scripted videos showing postal employees caught selling real estate in an office with rotary telephones, a mail carrier turning down a gift certificate to the restaurant he delivered to ("Sorry, ma'am, that would be a violation of federal law"), and cartoon videos about distracted driving ("Do you ever arrive at your destination and wonder, 'How did I get here?'"). On the last day of orientation, we all stood up, raised our right hands, and vowed to defend the Constitution.

Then was the week at Carrier Academy, where we practiced organizing fake mail in fake carrier cases. *Case* was a noun and a verb. The noun was a three-walled cubby filled with shelves and dividers representing the hundreds of addresses a single carrier delivered to in a day. The slots were arranged and labeled in order of delivery, and the cubby was just big enough for a carrier to reach every spot while standing in the middle. *To case* meant to use the case to put all unorganized mail into order of delivery. Several timed practices had us racing to case the mail, each of us trying to beat our previous time. Everyone was surprised when

I beat the experienced rural carrier who was transferring into the city. I wondered if I had been a mail carrier prodigy all this time. Esther would've loved that. As for my mother, I hadn't told her about my new job.

The trainees were guided into the parking lot, where an assortment of retired, rusty mailboxes were nailed onto equally beaten-up wooden posts. We took turns carrying a satchel of faded, falling-apart packages, holding a pile of worn magazines and flats, or larger letters, on our left arm, and at the same time gripping the fake letters from our case in our left hand, all while our right hand "fingered" the mail. How many mail carriers had trained on these items? What tone did these objects set for our service?

"*Walk* and look at the mail *at the same time!*" our trainer barked at us from the shade. To stand still while fingering the mail was an extravagant waste of time. We were to ready each address's mail during our approach, so we could drop in the bundle upon arrival, preparing the next address's mail as we moved.

"In real life, there will be bumps on the sidewalks, garden hedges, toys on the lawn—things to be mindful of as you walk and finger the mail."

For driver's training, we arrived on Saturday morning at seven A.M. at a much larger empty parking lot next to the mail-processing plant. We had five hours to learn how to drive the Long-Life Vehicle (LLV). There was an obstacle course with orange cones, fake mailboxes, and parallel-parking practice lines—which was nonsense because postal vehicles could double-park anywhere. We then had to drive through real streets and intersections, changing lanes and signaling, with the instructor trailing behind us. If we failed, we didn't get the job.

The right-side driver's seat was the biggest challenge. Everyone kept veering to the left. The LLVs also rattled loudly over every pebble and bump. They'd been commissioned by the military, where civilian comforts such as insulation were superfluous. The red, white, and blue stripes along the side evoked the nation-state, but the bumpers were childishly oversize, and the whole thing was pocked with dents and scratches. A sticker on the back perpetually announced: USPS IS HIRING!

While I drove, the gas gauge swung back and forth like a windshield wiper. I asked my driving instructor if my vehicle needed a repair, but he laughed. "They're all like that. Just fill up when the gas is at halfway when parked." At orientation, I'd heard stories of LLVs stranded in the middle of the freeway from an unexpectedly empty tank.

* * *

On my final day of training, I was to shadow a real mail carrier for a half day. It was a relief to be out of the processing plant, sitting shotgun in the Pro Van with Resy, an Indonesian mail carrier in her sixties who had the energy and laugh of a chipmunk, and the strength and softness of a Michelin Man. I hadn't gotten placed at Parkside but the adjacent Outer Richmond, another foggy neighborhood by the beach, only wealthier and with more commerce. At the station, I watched Resy organize and load her mail and packages. Other carriers jostled by saying:

"You're lucky—Resy is a good carrier. Very fast. But remember, she needs to buy you lunch today!"

"Resy, she's very good! Tell her to get you lunch."

Resy laughed like a chipmunk and said, "Then you give me your credit card!"

In fact, Resy had already picked up dim sum and tangerines on the way to work, along with a pair of work gloves that she told me to keep. The backs of the gloves had faces of angry pugs in white.

"They're really breathable and good grip."

I thanked her.

"I think I've seen you before," Resy said. "Do you go to church?"

"I used to." This was more personal information than I'd planned on sharing.

"Which one?"

"City Life."

"Is it the one that meets in the middle school?"

"Yes."

"I've visited before!"

A memory of Resy came to mind, not wearing her uniform and mail carrier hat, but a black wool coat, her smooth gray hair down and parted to the side. She was standing with her husband, a bald Russian man who also spoke with an accent. As a deaconess, I had greeted them, given them a Welcome Card to fill out, and signed them up for the next Welcome Lunch. I remembered wondering what it was like for their marriage to happen outside either of their mother tongues. This was years ago. I had also taught her granddaughters for a few weeks in children's Sunday school. They were shy, fair skinned, with long, curly light-brown hair. I felt like I knew too much about Resy.

I never wanted to see anyone from my school or church again. I didn't have the energy to perform my old self or explain the change, but I remembered my manners, forced a smile, and brightened my voice. "That's right. How are your granddaughters?"

"They're good! My oldest started high school."

"Oh, wow, time flies." I braced myself for her to say that her granddaughter went to San Francisco Christian School.

Instead, Resy asked, "Why don't you go to that church anymore?"

I thought about how to answer, but before I could, Resy asked me another question.

"Are you looking for a different church?"

I shrugged.

"Yeah, I remember my husband was bothered by something the pastor said at the Welcome Lunch, I can't remember what, but we never went back. I want my girls to grow up in a church community, but it's hard to find one we like. We tried Indonesian churches in the Peninsula, but they're too far away."

Church community. I remembered all the meal trains I organized for each new mother or church member who had just returned home from a hospital. Some meals I'd cooked and delivered myself, sometimes for people I'd met only once. On the other hand, when I needed to move, church folks came by to drop off boxes and shipping tape; a few days later, they arrived with vans and trucks. They hadn't let me help lift my own sofa.

And further back, in my childhood, our Korean church knew about my father's illness. Congregants gave our family discounted dentist appointments, oil changes, and tire rotations. Not to mention all the meals and food.

But when Esther died, my pastor tried to comfort me by recommending a four-hundred-page theological text called *The Fire That Consumes.* Its comfort was that instead of eternal conscious torment, God destroyed the soul of the unbeliever only once.

Only two people from church said, "I don't think Esther is in hell." Everyone else was forlorn and silent when I told them about my terror. Some even gave names of people they loved who might be in hell or were likely destined for hell. One of the people who wasn't worried about Esther said, "Maybe she had faith the size of a mustard seed." These posthumous attempts to bring Esther into compliance only angered me more. That wasn't who she was, and the whole premise was cruel. One mother said even though Esther was in hell, I should still love God, adding that she'd still love God if I ended up in hell, too. I snapped back that she was training her kids to love a God who committed spiritual genocide.

Which meant I had loved a God who committed spiritual genocide.

The one other congregant who didn't believe in hell introduced me to alternative atonement theories, which posited that Jesus's crucifixion was about conquering evil or paying a ransom to Satan, not absorbing God's wrath. Maybe if I had heard the theory earlier on, I might have found a way to cling to the faith, but by then I was sick of being the only one losing my mind. All of them had met Esther. They swallowed hell whole without throwing up.

"How long have you been working for the postal service?" I asked Resy.

"Has it already been thirty years? Wow, I'm getting old."

I kept up the shop talk. Resy told me that I had picked a good time to start—in the spring, after the rush of political mail for the local elections. "Spring and summer, really slow. Even if everyone goes on vacation, it's still so light. Perfect for learning. Not me. I started during Christmas."

"What's Christmas like?" When the subject of Christmas had come up, my trainers had lowered their voices and shaken their heads.

"Um, let's see . . . Well, when I had to watch my granddaughters because my daughter was on bed rest and her husband was overseas, I had a special deal with our supervisor. I started work at two A.M., so that at seven A.M., I could have my lunch break and take my granddaughters to school, and at five P.M., when I finished, I could pick them up from after-school, then go straight to bed while my husband made dinner. Everyone else started at the normal time, but they'd finish around midnight. I couldn't do that because my husband worked graveyard."

"How many days a week did you work like that?"

"Every single day in December. But overtime"—Resy rubbed her thumb against her fingers—"means a lot of dough."

I nodded and wondered what "a lot of dough" was to Resy. I pictured myself sleep-deprived, delivering mail in the middle of the night, maybe twisting an ankle on an acorn, and lying on the sidewalk, exhausted, and unable to get up. I felt a mix of dread and curiosity.

"You know what?" Resy went on. "I kind of like delivering mail at three in the morning. It's quiet. No traffic, completely empty. The only bad thing—sometimes dogs start barking, and I feel bad waking up customers."

We arrived at our first stop, a UPS store on Geary Boulevard.

"No, no! Stay in the van! You don't have to deliver anything today. Just watch."

I sat in the van while Resy made several trips into the UPS store, carrying boxes almost as big as herself plus several bins filled with smaller packages. I learned that though UPS, FedEx, and the USPS were competitors, they all took care of various legs for one another's deliveries. We used FedEx's planes and UPS's big rigs, and sometimes they used our mail carriers.

"So many toilet-paper and tissue orders these days," Resy said when she got back in the Pro Van. "And Clorox wipes. It's the corona."

She wiped her nose. "Oh, don't worry, it's just allergies! People look at me all scared now when I sneeze!" she said with a trill of giggles.

I nodded. I'd heard a story from Japan about a bus driver who never left the country and got the virus from a passenger. But that was Japan, which was close to China. The United States had a few cases in Seattle, New York, and that infected cruise ship docked in Oakland. All our infected people were quarantined. Resy probably didn't have the coronavirus.

3

On my first day, I got to Mendell Station at ten A.M.

I used to pray in moments like this. Supplications for God to be with me in a strange, new place. Because of my social anxiety, I used to pray before I met anyone—acquaintance, parents of students, students on the first days of school. *God, please be with me while I meet this person who is made in your image. Help me trust your loving purpose whether it is revealed today or not. Open my eyes to see what you want to teach me. Help me to love, to serve, or receive service with humility, so that your name may be glorified. Thank you for being the love that connects all people, and please help me not to sin against it.* Then I would be quiet and meditate on the universe brimming with God.

> Where can I go from your Spirit? Where can I flee from your presence?
> If I go up to the heavens, you are there; if I make my bed in depths, you are there.

If I rise on the wings of the dawn, if I settle on the far
side of the sea, even there your hand shall guide me, and
your right hand shall hold me fast.

But as I walked to my case, there were no prayers, no
presence.

The carrier annex was huge, with high ceilings and no
windows. A bit of sunlight entered through the door, a dimin-
ishing ray that barely made it past the first row of cases. The rest
of the annex was dimly lit with fluorescent panels high above the
carriers' heads. These lights were ugly but gentler on the eyes.
I was surrounded by an unfamiliar color palette—gray shelves,
blue pants and hats, orange and black plastic hampers, metal
cages, and dirty-white trays and bins—countless stimuli and
data to process and prioritize, responsibilities I did not fully
understand how I had come to bear. I had something vast to
navigate, each minute pressing into me in a way both discom-
fiting and animating, because people were asking me to do things
on a timeline that I couldn't dispute but only nod along to and
say, *Yes, I came here of my own accord. I agreed to perform.*

Instead of hours punctuated by bursts of *Help me, God* and
Thank you, God, emptiness rose to the surface. With each
aborted prayer was the question of whether anyone had ever
listened. Whether all the plaintive cries of people across the world
throughout history, during their most isolated and tortured
moments, had gone unheard.

*　*　*

"Hi, I'm Donna. What about you? Do you live in the city?"

"What's your name? Me, I'm José. Nice to meet you."

"Are you Chinese? . . . Oh, Korean? Your parents live here?"

"Are you married? Have any kids?"

"Hi, I'm Nico, your T6. Let me know if you have any questions."

A T6 was a relief carrier for six routes. They rotated around, delivering for regular carriers on their off days.

My co-workers' eyes twinkled, and they smiled easily. I gave monosyllabic answers with a polite smile. About 90 percent of them were immigrants, mostly Cantonese, but there were also several Mandarin speakers and Filipinos, as well as an Indonesian, a Thai, a Tibetan, a Salvadorean, a Samoan, a Greek, a Black, and two whites. The older immigrants were like aunties and uncles with their accents and corny jokes. It was hard to tell how old anyone was because they were all so tan and fit, but there were a handful of people in their twenties and two grandmas in their seventies.

I met my supervisor, Jyothi, a Nepalese woman with a ponytail down to her waist. She'd been a carrier until "becoming a supervisor made me fat." When other carriers saw me training with Resy, one of them muttered that Resy was the real supervisor. Then Jyothi asked Resy how to break up the open routes (a route without anyone to deliver it that day) into several overtime assignments to be split among several carriers. Resy's dramatic pauses and wagging finger showed she enjoyed being asked for advice.

Manwai pushed a hamper past me without a glance, and a carrier standing by my case muttered to me that Manwai had the easiest, shortest route in the whole station and, on top of that, never did a lick of overtime. The carrier next to the mutterer nodded with an expression that might have been disdain or resignation. Manwai's wiry frame, hooked nose, and hunched posture made him look like a Chinese Mr. Burns, and I did a double take when I heard his voice for the first time—a velvety baritone.

Ayesha from the case next to mine introduced herself. A young Black woman with almond-shaped eyes and long lashes. Her hair was pulled into a tight bun. She was around my height, around my age. I imagined her at my high school. She gave off student council vibes. Ayesha had been a carrier for three months, the second newest after me. Like me, she had been placed on an open route of a carrier on extended injury leave.

Everyone besides Manwai found a reason to pass by my case and say hello. Thankfully, no one could linger for long. Everyone had work to do.

4

I met Esther when we were fourteen. Tall, tan, skinny, loud, and thick-haired with a loping gait, she asked if she could get a ride home after a tennis match, having learned we lived three blocks apart in Torrance, outside Los Angeles. I tried to think of an excuse for saying no, but I couldn't, and enough seconds passed for it to get awkward before I gave in. On the way home, my narcoleptic mother was falling asleep at the wheel again. Each time we swerved dangerously close to cars, they honked at us, and Esther shouted or muttered under her breath. None of this was enough to fully wake my dozing mother. I stayed silent, but when we drove up onto the sidewalk and back down, I shrieked alongside Esther. With a crazed look in her eyes, my mother screamed louder at me in Korean, *"How can I concentrate when you're making so much noise?"* I couldn't tell if it was worse that Esther, who was also Korean, understood what my mother had said.

My mother forgot Esther was in the car and parked in front of our own building without dropping Esther off. Esther simply got out of the car and said, "It's okay, I can walk from here."

I ran after her. "I'm so sorry," I said when I caught up. "My mom drives crazy. She doesn't always." I was terrified what Esther might tell other people at school and needed to gauge what she intended to do with this information so that I could adequately brace myself. I felt small, at Esther's mercy.

Esther turned to me with a sheepish smile. "Your family's fucked up, too."

Her smile was the bridge on which we met. She reached out to the very thing that isolated me and threatened to shame me. I felt a handshake in her kind eyes.

After that memorable ride, I told my mom she didn't need to pick me up after school anymore. Esther had asked if I wanted to walk home with her. The forty-five minutes felt short because we talked the entire time, interrupting each other repeatedly before parting ways. We snickered about our perverted tennis coach and our TTH (trying too hard) teammates, commented on the shops we walked by, planned classes to take together. We bought and split fries. We opened up about our family dramas. Esther never flinched at anything I said about my dad's illness or my mother's strictness, nor did I when she told me about her dad's drinking or her brothers' illegal shenanigans. We flitted back and forth between the serious and the light without interrupting the flow of chatter. I hadn't realized how much I had to say until I met Esther.

One day, after a couple of weeks of walking home together, Esther invited me over. Her house was in a cul-de-sac, two-story, with a three-car garage and neatly trimmed topiary in the front. The sharply slanted wooden awning over the entrance felt like a statement. At fourteen, before I had seen inside the homes of the wealthy near Stanford, I was impressed.

As soon as I walked in, I could hear Esther's brothers playing video games. Her mother looked like Esther but older, less goofy, more elegant. They had the same small face and crowded teeth. Her brothers' laughter and bickering over the sound of machine guns filled the house, so upstairs, Esther cranked her music even louder. She could have shut her bedroom door, but at the time it felt as though the house ran on noise energy. I marveled that her mom was okay with this. We had to shout to be heard, but mostly we listened to music, what Esther derived the most pleasure from and wanted to share with me. Esther played Sleater-Kinney, Scout Niblett, Electrelane, and Cat Power. She also showed me her zine collection and mock-ups of her own efforts. She asked if I wanted to make one with her. A new world opened up before me. Unlike the twinkling, catchy K-pop melodies about falling in love and endless devotion with which I'd grown up, her music sounded unrehearsed, like a satisfying release of pent-up discomfort. Rather than finesse or diva moves, there was sure-footed repetition. Even with its delays and cracked voices, everything fit into place.

Once, an older brother walked by and said, "You know this doesn't make you cool." Esther got up and closed the door. She seemed mildly irritated, but I wondered if siblings had a unique way of checking each other's egos. For all of Esther's expertise and passion, there wasn't a hint of snobbery.

Soon I heard the distant sound of a car door shutting. Esther's music, the arguing, laughing, machine guns, and car crashes downstairs went silent as if someone had pulled a plug. Her dad was home early. Esther confessed that technically, according to house rules, no one was allowed to come over. The plan, Esther whispered while her dad crossed the front lawn, was to wait for the right moment for me to sneak out. A finger to her lips, Esther pushed me into her closet and gently closed the door on my face.

Esther had told me that when her dad was drunk, he was mostly just sullen and keeled over. He did his most fucked-up things when sober. Her brothers got the worst of it, and all of them knew Esther was her dad's favorite. Only she could get away with scolding him, though she had to do it sparingly since one could only poke a bear so many times.

In her closet, I smelled dirty laundry. Stacks of magazines were slippery under my feet. I worried about Esther, who was out there facing her dad. But I was also used to being invisible while waiting for an ugly moment to pass.

The closet door opened, and I had to adjust my eyes to the light. Esther grabbed my hand, and we tiptoed downstairs to the front door. Esther's brothers were out of sight, but at the bottom of the staircase by the entrance, I turned my head and caught the backside of Esther's dad, just outside the sliding glass door by the kitchen, smoking alone in the backyard. I thought of God showing Moses His backside. Esther pushed me out and shut the door silently behind me.

I looked down and saw my backpack in my hand. Esther must have put it there because I didn't remember grabbing it.

It was Esther's shoving and pulling me out of her closet that gave me the confidence to invite her over to my own home, a one-bedroom apartment by the freeway. I hadn't invited anyone over since my eighth birthday party, when my mother had ignored all my friends and muttered nonstop to herself in the kitchen. I had tried to distract my friends with nail polish or games of MASH, but they still asked if they could go home early, before the pizza arrived.

"Oh good, you're here," my mother said in Korean as we walked in. My mother was wearing a black trench coat, purple leopard-print scarf, and large sunglasses and carrying a thick blue canvas bag covered in stains. She was a compact, pale woman with tattooed eyebrows and eyeliner. When possible, she preferred to endure costly pain once rather than repeatedly purchase makeup or draw on her face. She had a similar approach to child discipline. A single powerful demonstration—such as digging her high heel into my foot under the table at a restaurant for divulging family issues—made her point clear. It seemed to have worked because I was a well-behaved child. On the other hand, caring for my dad—helping him to the bathroom, bathing him, moving his muscles, bringing him food—had no shortcuts, and she saw them as her duties to God alone.

Esther and I took off our shoes by the door.

"Mom, this is Esther. We're going to do homework together." I knew my mother would not remember giving Esther a ride.

Esther bowed, and her *annyeonghaseyo* was doubly distorted by her Kyongsang dialect and American accent.

My mother nodded. *"I see you can't speak our language."*

Esther retorted, "What about your English, *ajumma*?"

I whipped my head to face my mother. I would never have dared speak to her like that. To my shock, a smile crept over her face. Somehow, Esther was the only one who could elicit those rare smiles or laughs.

My mother turned to me. *"I'm off."*

"Do you want to say hi to my dad?" I asked Esther after my mom left. I had already told her about his muscular dystrophy, which had started when I was one and left him increasingly bedridden. Our family lived by faith and several forms of government assistance—my father's disability checks, my mother's caregiver support checks, Section 8 housing, and food stamps. Then there was my mother's side hustle, dyeing church-women's hair in their homes (cash only, lest the government take away its assistance for our having too much money).

I knocked quietly on my parents' bedroom door. "*Appa*, this is my friend Esther."

My dad was lying on his side, sporting shaggy sideburns and a mullet, overdue for a haircut. In his hands was one of his old Buddhist philosophy books he kept hidden under the bed. He took them out when my mom wasn't home. These "books from college," as he called them, offered him helpful ideas for chronic pain, which he translated into Christian thought. For instance, instead of the self not existing because it was an illusion, he said he had no self outside of God, who was real. But I wondered if he said this so I wouldn't rat him out for reading idolatrous texts. Why keep them hidden under his bed in a closed box if he wasn't doing anything wrong?

The whole room smelled like his musk. He was clean-shaven at least.

Esther repeated the loud, happy hello. My dad smiled and propped himself up on an elbow. They exchanged pleasantries—in Korean he asked her name, how she knew me—all questions that Esther answered in English, in her bouncy manner. He seemed amused. The incongruity of her bright, ringing voice in my apartment made me realize that my family spoke in hushed tones.

When my dad nodded and slowly laid himself back down, I tiptoed out of the room with Esther and closed the door behind us.

Esther looked around. "Where do you sleep?"

"In the living room. See?" I opened a hallway closet and gestured at the blankets I pulled out at night to sleep on the floor. They were thick and heavy, covered in colorful silk.

"What about your stuff? Your clothes?"

I told her there was a separate small dresser in my parents' room and some space in my parents' closet. There was also a small desk in the living room where I kept my books and school things.

"You don't have any space that's your own?"

"My space is everywhere, a little bit."

Esther nodded. We sat down at the coffee table in the living room and did our history homework.

There was a knock on the door. I answered it and bowed to a woman holding a stack of containers wrapped in fabric.

"Is your mother home?"

"She stepped out for a moment."

"Here, put this in the fridge. Tell her Sister Hong stopped by. Your poor mother never shows how much she's suffering. I've never met someone with such deep faith in the Lord. I receive so much grace because of your mother's silent, suffering example. She's just like Jesus. Listen to your mother."

I thanked her, accepted the gift with both hands, bowed, and closed the door. In the containers were vegetable pancakes, marinated eggplant, and a radish-and-beef soup. I put them in the fridge and folded the cloth into a neat square. On my way back to the coffee table, I grabbed a large Fuji apple, a small cutting board, a knife, and two tiny forks.

"What was that?" Esther asked.

As I peeled and cut the apple, I explained how church people visited and brought food on account of my dad. My mother secretly detested these visits and only endured them because she considered doing so to be part of her service to God and His people, training in humility and self-denial. I said that my mother confessed many times that if it weren't for her faith, she would have run away or killed herself. Thus, I was not to feel thankful to my mom, but to God, for giving her the strength to take care of us. But I knew Esther didn't go to church, and my heart pounded as I said all of this aloud to an outsider for the first time.

Esther was fascinated. "So, you don't think your mom loves you?"

"God gives her the love." If anyone asked me what love looked like at that time, I would have pointed to Christ's body bleeding on the cross.

"But she wouldn't love you without God."

"None of us would love without God," I said quietly. Normally I wouldn't have said anything because Esther was a nonbeliever. No one knew me in all of my self-contained spaces—my one-bedroom apartment, my Korean church, my American public school—no one except for God. Part of why I loved God so much was because God knew every version of me. Nothing was embarrassing or weird to Him. He abided through it all. Despite my family's close calls—eviction notices, my mom's kidney rupturing, the multiple near car accidents—there was always unexpected help that saved us in a way we could never have mustered on our own. To attribute it all to our own goodness and ability would be boorish ingratitude, an affront to God.

Esther was the first human—my age, at my school, in my neighborhood—who I wished could know me in all my separate realms.

"Well, we're friends, and that has nothing to do with God," she said.

"How do you know?"

Esther thought about it. "I don't know. I just think we're the ones who decided to be friends."

Such a degree of choice and responsibility seemed too small to describe what was happening. "Then how did we meet or live three blocks apart? How were we able to understand each other when we talked?"

Esther laughed. "You make it sound such a miracle."

I blushed. I had never met someone I felt so comfortable and excited to be around. "I don't know, I thank God for you. And I ask God to bless you and protect you."

"That sounds nice." Then she admitted, "I do wonder what all this is for."

"All what?"

She looked around the room, then out the window, which showed telephone poles, wires, and the sky. "All of this. Life."

I thought of her parents, who fought so much the neighbors called the police. I thought of how hard she struggled to hold her own in that house, of her obsession with music and her eagerness to share it, of how she fell asleep in the sun in her backyard until all her limbs turned red and she looked like a cooked lobster. She wondered what it was all for.

I answered, "'The chief end of man is to glorify God and enjoy Him forever.'"

Esther laughed. Then she squeezed me so tightly it hurt because she was bony. I relaxed into her grip because her hug was what mattered.

5

Resy treated me like a little niece. She was also my On-the-Job Instructor (OJI) and was to supervise my first three days of delivering mail. In the morning, she let me finish organizing her mail while she loaded her packages. Before delivering anything, she bought me lunch at Superior Palace, as she did for every new carrier she trained. (We both ordered the pork and bitter melon.) She said she liked the restaurant because they always remembered her husband's shrimp allergy.

Back out on the neighborhood, she showed me a trick of using the edge of the magazine or letter to lift the cover of a mailbox and push in the mail in one smooth motion. At Carrier Academy, I was taught to use a knuckle to lift and hold open the mailbox, then turn my wrist to push in the mail. I saw how Resy's technique shaved off a few seconds, but it was difficult to replicate. She laughed with pride when she saw me struggling and told me the knuckle way worked just fine.

I was let off early my first day of delivering. They only gave me half a route. Once I delivered at standard speed, they'd give me three fourths, then the full route.

On my drive home, my mind snagged on an idea. I never got to say goodbye to Esther. At once, I felt as if I were hearing about her death for the first time, slapped in the back of the head by the absurdity of her permanent absence.

My mind kept going where I didn't want it to go, the psalmist confessing to God, "You have kept count of how many times I toss in my sleep; put my tears in your bottle. Are they not in your book?"

The presence of God—a divine, cosmic witness—used to hush whatever caused my tears. It didn't matter that nothing was fixed. As long as God knew what I was going through, watching me, bottling my tears, and counting my tossings, that was enough. God had been my divine witness, Esther my human witness, and both were gone.

With the concrete overpass winding above me and silent shipyards to my right, I was alone. No one was watching me. No one knew what I was going through. Then I imagined maybe Esther was like God, looking down on not only me but her family, our friends, knowing our thoughts, bottling our tears, and writing them down in her book. But this was a fantasy, and it gave way.

At home, Dolmangi saw me through my window to the back-yard. He yawned and crawled out of the doghouse that Esther and I had assembled. His little tap dance at the door showed his enthusiasm to come back into the apartment. I brought his food and water bowl in as well. I wondered if he knew, through smell or intuition, that Esther was dead. At my kitchen counter, I ate the almond-butter, apricot-jam sandwich I had packed for lunch. With nothing to do and nervous energy to expel, I walked Dolmangi until his curly tail began to sag from exhaustion. Then I wrote Esther a letter, like we used to in high school. We had the same history teacher in different periods, so each of us would tape our letters to the bottom of the desk that we shared for the other to read. At the beginning of each history class, I lightly felt underneath my desk, avoiding old bumps of chewing gum and dried boogers, until I found her letter wedged between the wood and the metal. I'd surreptitiously write her a response in class, fold the paper, and secure it in the same spot.

I imagined this was only a momentary separation, a distance that could still be breached.

> Esther,
>
> I keep wanting to tell you about the postal service and how unrecognizable my life has become, but then I remember you're dead, and that's what got me in this fucking twilight zone. You would've liked my station with all the blue-collar immigrants and cheesy jokes. Hard workers who don't take themselves too seriously, like you.
>
> I miss you every day. I don't know where you are or if you are. I worry about you.
>
> I miss you sitting in my kitchen reading aloud from your diary while I cooked for us. The warmth of the stove, your voice, your thoughts. You ate my food even when I burned or oversalted it, as if it were delicious. Did you resent that I took that for granted? I wish I cooked more carefully for you.
>
> I love you forever. If you still exist, I hope you are happy, at peace, and not alone.

That night I dreamed I was in Esther's apartment room, stripped bare except for a pair of her old jeans on the floor. In my dream, I took off my pants and tried putting on hers, but they were doll-size and wouldn't fit. I bawled in frustration. I walked toward the window that faced the stoop. Even though Esther's apartment was on the second floor, she was standing on the other side of the dirty window. She was backlit by a light so bright I could barely see her laughing at my attempt to fit into her jeans. She looked sympathetic. I said nothing. I knew she wasn't able to speak to me, no matter how much I missed her voice. But she looked so happy, perhaps a little pained. I stared ravenously at her face.

I gave up trying to sleep and sat up in the dark. I stumbled into the kitchen, opened a sparkling water, then changed my mind about it. I wrote her another letter.

Esther,
I remember the day we cleaned out your apartment. When your dad, your brothers, and I stepped out of your room into the hallway with garbage bags full of your stuff, your mom screamed. We all heard it, but we respected her for waiting until all of us were out of the room, out of her sight. We just kept walking quietly to the rented van. Her scream resonated with the one in my chest while also being incomprehensible and beyond me. Did you hear it where you are? I hope not. If I wished you hadn't, why am I telling you now? Because no matter how hard I try, I have no certainty that you hear my thoughts anymore. Or because I am so used to telling you everything that I don't know how to stop.

Our friends told me how good I was to help your family during their visit to San Francisco, taking them to the spot where you died, helping them pick up your backpack from the police station, gathering our friends to meet with them, coordinating the tree-planting ceremony, helping write your obituary, faxing your death certificate to your work. You know what's crazy? I tried as hard as I did because a part of me believed that if I helped your family with the logistics of your death, it would bring you back. I knew it made no sense, but once the idea was there, I couldn't stop spending every ounce of energy I had to help your parents and brothers. I needed to pay off whatever cosmic debt took you away. I was willing to do everything your death required—if only you could please come back.

I folded up both letters and put each in a separate envelope. On the envelopes I wrote her childhood address on the front right; I wrote mine in the top left corner. I peeled a stamp for each envelope and stuck it onto the top right corner, as all Americans had been taught in elementary school. I wondered if they learned how to write emails now.

I took out my phone and scrolled through my pictures until I found the one that I'd taken of Esther months ago at the beach. She was so backlit by the bright sky, the sparkling ocean, and the shining wet sand that it was hard to see her. She wore a black sweatshirt, faded jeans, and clogs, as one did at a San Francisco beach. She was repulsed by anything egotistical, but this didn't mean she lacked flair—hoop earrings, rings, tinted lip balm, and the occasional tattoo she gave herself and her friends. In the picture, her grin displayed both rows of teeth, and her hands were in her backpack, in the middle of taking something out. Did Esther visit me in my dream to reassure me she was okay, or did my brain recycle this image?

I took out my Sharpie and wrote *dec* on the front of the envelopes, which was a return-to-sender abbreviation for "deceased." I also crossed out each stamp with the Sharpie, which we were supposed to do when the machines forgot to postmark them.

I put both letters in my satchel.

6

On the second day, Resy watched me deliver mail again. As we were walking back to our vehicles, I received a citywide text message from the mayor of San Francisco: *Due to COVID-19, shelter-in-place will begin on Tuesday, March 17th, 2020. Only essential work and travel will be allowed.*

"Did you see this? Do we have to stay home next week?" My fingers holding the mail went numb. I didn't want to be stuck in my apartment. I also wanted to finish my three-month probation so I could get the cute uniform instead of the mesh vest with the USPS logo. It was the only thing I looked forward to.

Resy laughed with a wave of the hand. "Of course not. We delivered during anthrax." I detected a little pride when she said this. Grinning like a proud auntie, she said, "You're a quick learner, and we're a fast station, so I think you'll fit right in."

Ever since Resy had told me that small sips of water meant fewer trips to the bathroom, I'd been drinking from Esther's old, dented Nalgene (from the animal shelter where she'd volunteered) and not peeing for eight hours. The more time spent delivering, the better. I noticed all the carriers had an enormous water jug in their truck—Resy's was a repurposed plastic milk gallon. I never wondered where mail carriers went pee, but now I knew it was public park bathrooms. They were clean, but that was irrelevant to me.

I asked, "Are you worried about the coronavirus, Resy?"

"Well, how many cases are in SF? Less than a hundred. The mayor's just being safe. I'm sure it won't last long."

*   *   *

My third day on the job, and the first day of quarantine, I was to deliver a whole route.

"She can case her own mail," I overheard Resy telling Jyothi at the supervisor's desk.

I preemptively tried to memorize my case for a full five minutes. It was the sort of thinking I craved:

Fulton Street on the bottom left shelf.

The 700 block of Twenty-eighth Avenue on the bottom middle and right middle, first even, then odd.

The 700 block of Twenty-ninth Avenue, even then odd, bottom right, and middle left.

The 800 block of Twenty-ninth Avenue, second row left . . .

I swiveled my body left to right, turned my head up and down, trying to internalize the exact position of my body and neck for each set of numbers and streets. Then I started putting each stray letter and flat from my hot case into the correct slot. Hot case was the mail that the machines had missed, that needed to be sequenced by hand.

I thought of stories I enjoyed as a child, the details writers deemed worthy of slowing down time to describe. After I quit teaching, I found myself reaching for *Anne of Green Gables*, *Little Women*, *Little House in the Big Woods*, baffled that I should be craving children's stories as an adult. In these books, women and children were relegated to small spaces bursting at the seams, tiny details filled with weight and gravity, their secret, private earthquakes. A young daughter obsessively watching her father make bullets, the step-by-step directions—how tempting it was for the girl to touch the small, glistening black balls that would burn her. Or the descriptions of the fit, fabric, and adornments of a new dress and how it felt to wear. The grand feasts that were only grand to them, in their poverty. These details were as soothing as bits of oceans sinking into the sand. Reading about these characters' lives turned me into a witness, someone important. And the characters became important because they had a witness. It was a sort of dignity.

When my mind felt close to thinking about Esther's death, hell, and God, I filled it instead with cases, shelves, hampers, cages, trucks, carts, ropes, trays, and tubs. All the equipment seemed built to survive the apocalypse and was thrown about, dropped, and bumped around in a way that proved its durability. Though upon closer inspection, I saw glimpses of the original yellow or blue paint—the cheery beginnings. The equipment had seen things. But each tool worked well enough, quietly delivering a large mound of mail and packages each day.

My co-workers' uniforms had gray spots from rubbing constantly against the mail that they held to their torsos. The stains didn't come out, they said, no matter how often the uniforms were washed.

Soft denim pouches nailed into each case held rubber bands.

Cats lounged in the employee parking lot. Someone left water bowls by the tree planters, and the cats drank from them, sat and stared with their yellow eyes. They slunk out from under the cars to lie in the sun between the bumpers. Resy joked that all the cats loitering in the parking lot wanted a job at the postal service.

I found myself comforted, comfortable. A suspicious voice inside my head questioned this comfort, but I was too tired to give it more consideration.

"Hey, Miriam." Resy snapped me out of my reverie. "You're going to get caught if you leave your yellows out like that. Always case these first." She grabbed my yellow tray—the tray that held machine-sequenced flats (magazines and larger envelopes) and stacked my flats on the table. Then she snatched up the tray. For unknown reasons, yellow trays were supposed to be loaded directly into our vehicles and not allowed into the office.

"Some people throw it away." She dipped the yellow flat into the trash bin. "But me, I just take it back." She took it away with her.

"Thanks, Resy," I called out.

Machines now sequenced most flats and letters into the order of delivery. Before the machines were invented, mail carriers spent most of their days sorting mail—four hours in the office and two on the streets. The skill took time to learn. Vets cased at light speed, and newcomers cased like slugs. This became important during the famous mail carrier strike of 1970 during the Civil Rights Movement, when most mail carriers were Black. Strikes were illegal for federal employees, but working conditions were dismal, unsafe, and paid a pittance. Mail carriers in Manhattan walked out after Congress gave themselves a 41 percent raise and gave mail carriers 5 percent. The rest of the country's carriers followed suit or threatened to join if any striking carrier was punished. The stock market nearly closed. Paychecks, bills, and Vietnam War draft notices were held up, so Nixon sent in the National Guard. At orientation, union representatives had shown us black-and-white footage of confused military men scratching their buzz-cut heads, standing in front of old carrier cases with mountains of jumbled letters. They couldn't do it.

The strike lasted eight days before mail carriers got what they asked for. In the same footage, one saw the majestic and commanding post office buildings, almost as distinguished as the city halls, in the downtown of every major city. Despite that the strike disrupted everyone's lives, the public backed the mail carriers. At orientation, our trainer said mail carriers to this day enjoyed widespread popular support and high approval ratings. I wondered who was conducting those polls and why. Though, it wasn't hard to imagine people saying, "Yeah, sure, I like my mail carrier." In whatever the weather, mail carriers' brief daily presence was a combination of dependability and a bit of excitement—*Did anything come for me?* And everyone knew those uniforms were cute.

Now with email, private parcel-delivery companies, and automatic sorting, a mail carrier strike would be much less catastrophic. We only cased what the machines missed, for about half an hour, and there were far more packages to organize. Inside the station, everyone broke the rules and brought in the yellow trays and cased the flats, so we could carry one pile of flats instead of two. Most carriers also brought in the letter trays, which also weren't allowed inside, to mark off each block with rubber bands or some other method. The majority of rules from the carrier handbook were routinely broken due to their complete impracticality on the streets.

Then I remembered my trainer at Carrier Academy telling us *not* to break protocol during probation, even if everyone else was, because if we were caught, we could get fired. But to follow the handbook seemed unbearably inefficient. I flagged down Manwai, who was walking by my case, wanting to hear his baritone voice. "Am I too new to be casing my flats? Or am I allowed to break the rules?"

"Break them all. Except when the manager or postmaster is nearby. Actually, sometimes I follow the rules and slow myself down on purpose."

"Why?"

"Because the handbook is used to arbitrate labor disputes. They can't say nothing if I followed every one of their goddamn rules. The handbook hasn't been updated since 1976—before the days of automatic sorting. If they want to get mad at me for delivering slow, tell them to update the handbook. The postal service is run by a bunch of idiots. Just look at our stupid deals with Amazon and UPS. Usually we charge more for heavier packages, but with Amazon and UPS, it's one cheap flat rate, a little over a dollar. So a fifty-pound package that's taller than you, which takes time to load, unload, and carry, is calculated the same as a tiny package that you can shove in your satchel. Amazon and UPS have trained businessmen to work out a deal, and we have former mail carriers promoted to admin. We get screwed."

The satisfaction in listening to Manwai's tirade reminded me of my conversations with Esther. She had lacked a filter for both of us while I tried to cultivate meekness and gratitude. Was bitterness now accessible to me?

"Don't listen to anything he says," Resy interrupted, stopping with her hamper.

I smiled, expecting her to be joking, but her face was stern.

Manwai turned away with his heavy hamper rumbling on the floor, his face hardened.

"I don't have time to complain because I have packages to deliver," Resy went on after he'd left. "Miriam, this is a good station. We deliver in a nice neighborhood. You don't want to work in the Tenderloin with the smell of pee and the druggies waiting by your mail truck, or in the Bayview, where mail carriers get picked on by gangs as a part of their initiations. Jyothi can tell who's a good carrier, and she'll fight for anyone she believes in. I can tell you're a keeper. So don't listen to Manwai. He should have retired years ago." Resy rolled her hamper in the opposite direction without another word. It was normal for conversations to end abruptly because we all had work to do.

Within minutes, another carrier speed-walked over and said, "Angelo's here."

"Who?"

"Manager."

Even though Resy had taken away the incriminating evidence of my yellow trays, I still had all my letter trays stacked on my stool. I covered them with my jacket and satchel and slipped outside with my hamper to load my vehicle. On my way out, I noted that Angelo was a heavyset Filipino with glasses. The one I couldn't break the rules in front of.

*   *   *

Spent from all the hyperactivity of the morning, my mind was blissfully silent on my drive to my route.

Except the freeway was abandoned. I'd never seen the lanes of the 101 empty as far I could see. Only a few mail trucks puttered in a row. I didn't signal to change lanes. When I got off the freeway, I obeyed the meaningless traffic lights so as to not embarrass the lights. Main arteries of the city—Lincoln

Way, Nineteenth Avenue through Golden Gate Park, Fulton Street, usually filled with stop-and-go traffic—were as quiet as the sky above. The lockdown. I involuntarily recalled a passage from Isaiah:

> And there will be a highway
> called the Way of Holiness.
> The unclean will not travel it—
> only those who walk in the Way—
> and fools will not stray onto it.
> No lion will be there,
> And no vicious beast will go up on it.
> Such will not be found there,
> But the redeemed will walk upon it.

*   *   *

There were no redeemed in San Francisco that morning. Only workers who had recently found out they were essential. Every once in a while, on the empty streets, I'd see an ambulance or a lone Toyota or Honda, probably being driven by a supermarket clerk, sanitation worker, or nurse. There was no chance to gloat in the unanimous acknowledgment that without us, society would crumble. For all the "hero" talk, we weren't paid an extra cent or asked if we even wanted to do this. In the praise of essential workers, I heard underlying guilt: our working conditions were becoming hazardous, but no one wanted to compensate us for the risks, and everyone needed us to take them. Our exposure to the virus was deemed unavoidable, even acceptable, for everyone else's sake. The ones on the empty highways were neither holy nor redeemed.

The world mirrored my disaster. The folks staying safe at home were chosen and blessed. On the day the streets cleared, I found myself caught outside. I kept seeing an image in my mind: a wall with no end in any direction—east, west, up to the sky, down into the earth. I was condemned to walk alongside it, searching for an opening I'd never find. I didn't know whether to cry or curl up on the ground and sleep.

Why were only some people saved? Why didn't everyone reach old age? Why were some stuck outside? These things were not decided by moral superiority, personal value, or worth. I was nostalgic for when I was on the other side of that wall, in the cocoon of security, with praise of God on my lips.

Another part of me knew that going back to God was no longer an option. I thought of children stuck at home with abusive parents, now without the reprieve of school during the day. Day laborers, cooks, servers, and hotel workers with no access to employment or unemployment checks. To be enclosed within strong walls was not a haven for everyone—for some, it was suffocating.

What would Esther have made of this?

*   *   *

Usually, the station was quieter and darker at the day's end because carriers returned their trucks to the lot at different times. Many went home after parking and dropping off their outgoing mail, though a few ate snacks in their cases, draining the clock.

But on the first day of quarantine, carriers lingered and convened in the dim station, chatting about the emptiness of the streets.

"It feels like the summer. I don't need to dodge kids and cars by the schools."

"More time to nap in my truck."

"No traffic, no rush to finish on time."

Some of the carriers huddled together and spoke in Cantonese or Mandarin. They looked concerned, and then one would say something in a grim tone that made the others laugh.

The CDC was adamant that the general population not wear surgical or N95 masks, telling us to save them for healthcare professionals. An older Chinese carrier passed out cloth masks to everyone at the station. Each Ziploc bag contained one cloth mask and a tiny piece of paper with English and Chinese script. The English said the masks had been sewn by a nonprofit for the use of Chinese newcomers. I wasn't its intended recipient, so I hesitated. "Go ahead, take it," the carrier said. "They gave me a lot. They have a lot." I chose a light-blue-and-yellow tie-dye.

I looked over at the small box of surgical masks on our supervisor Jyothi's desk. There weren't enough for all of us, so my co-workers with gray and white hair got dibs.

"My sister lives in Indonesia," Resy told me. "She can't leave the house and their grocery stores are empty. She asked me to mail her Indonesian ramen and spices from here!"

I was young and healthy, but I worked alongside thirty people for two hours in the morning. There were YouTube videos with elaborate steps on how to disinfect the groceries and packages that we delivered. I pondered the angry pugs on my gloves— would they protect me from the virus?

In a different life, I was teaching a Scripture class online from my computer. Organizing grocery trips for the elderly in our congregation. Asking Esther about the rules of our bubble. How did I end up here?

When I walked Dolmangi after dinner, the streets were filled with an inordinate number of pedestrians with scarves hanging on their chins. When any of them approached each other, they covered the lower halves of their faces with the scarf, letting it fall again after they passed. The new, choreographed dance of unessential workers.

7

On Amazon Sundays there was no church, but the six most junior carriers, including Ayesha, my case neighbor, delivered parcels for Amazon and UPS. No mail. Everyone else rested.

We were the youngest carriers in the station, except for a dad in his fifties who'd come to the States from China and started working for the postal service five years before. The combined energy of the Cantonese-speaking men reminded me of Esther's brothers. I didn't mind my lack of understanding because I enjoyed how fluidly they spoke, how relaxed they looked, how much they made each other laugh. Among themselves, in Cantonese, they guffawed with their chests, as if luxuriating in the quiet and space. With me, in English, they spoke haltingly, still friendly but not so loose. Something was lost.

Movies and shows made clowns out of people with accents, exaggerating their clumsiness and pent-up emotions, but to me, accents signaled the intelligence and resilience of surviving in a non-native language. Though every one of their words exposed their vulnerability, they refused to be silent and forced themselves to overcome their embarrassment. Their accents allowed me to let go of the desire to be irreproachable and evoked my desire to convey respect. There was also the cozy familiarity of it—my parents, aunts, uncles, and grandparents all spoke English with accents.

I caught myself. I was viewing my co-workers through a warm, rosy lens but was reluctant to get to know them. My voyeurism kept them at a sterile distance, interpreting them without giving them a chance to respond. I should have known better. I resisted having pretend conversations with Esther in my head because no matter how well I knew her, she said things I couldn't predict.

Perhaps the older immigrant co-workers saw me, a child of immigrants, as the opposite of what they wanted their children to become—themselves. I wondered if they had family in China.

I asked them if any had worked at other stations before Mendell Station, Zone 21.

All of them except Ayesha and me.

"Yeah, I got moved many times a month when I started out," one carrier said.

"Many times a month?" said the man next to him. "Every morning I got a call—a new station, different part of the city."

"Zone Two, next to us, so crazy," said another. "Downtown is hectic, one-way streets, all those cyclists. You step in shit and can't tell if it's dog or human."

"I don't know, I liked Zone Two. Something crazy happens every day. It's like delivering mail in a video game."

"Which stations are the best to work in?" I asked.

"Actually, our zone is really good. Residential, quiet, clean. Lots of carriers try to transfer here. That's why we have fast carriers. Only the best can stay."

"Which station is the worst?"

"Townsend."

"Definitely Townsend."

"Townsend is hell."

"What's so bad about Townsend?" I asked.

"Not enough people. People always screaming at each other."

"Really heavy mail. Confusing, crowded streets. Everything is backed up. Nothing gets delivered on time."

"Some of their routes is just one block of skyscrapers. That's it for the whole day. I guess you don't have to walk a lot."

"I'd rather walk."

"True. Because every day someone is crying in Townsend."

"But everyone cries when they start the postal service."

"They do?" I asked.

"You're lucky. Zone Twenty-one from the beginning *and* not moving around. *And* staying on one route? I wish!"

*   *   *

Out in the parking lot where we loaded our vehicles, a young Cantonese guy with a Mohawk and sloping shoulders came to inspect my truck. I was inside the back of the vehicle, squatting between the shelves as I read the addresses on my packages and placed them in coherent piles. With one hand he held the top of the large opening in the back of the vehicle. He kept the other on his slim waist.

"Hi." I paused with a package in my hands, as still as a squirrel holding an acorn, waiting for him to reveal the reason for his visit. His eyes scanned the shelves—left, top, bottom, then me in the middle. Then right, top, bottom, again his eyes on me.

"How many routes you got?"

"Three."

He smiled. "That's it?"

"James told me to start with three and let him know if I had room." He nodded. "How many do you have?" I asked him back, not wanting to seem distant and impolite, though the effort pained me.

"Me? We all have five."

"Ayesha, too?" Ayesha was driving an LLV as I was, instead of the larger Pro Van.

"Nah. Ayesha has three—like you."

I wondered if he'd visited her truck.

"You can turn your packages around. Fill the top of the shelves more." He began rotating my packages, so they took up less space, then piled the parcels atop one another until they squished against the roof. "If you pack them like this, they won't fall when you make a turn. Plus, more space."

"Oh, wow, thank you."

"No problem." He walked away.

Co-workers would notice and correct my ignorance about the details that my training and handbook didn't address. For example, when one of my packages leaked and spilled liquid, an older co-worker stepped away from his own work to show me how to cover it with a clear plastic bag so that I could still scan the barcode. He found and handed me the stamp that told the customer we'd received the package broken. He advised that I deliver it first to get it out of the way, before he walked away to finish casing his own mail. No one hesitated to put down his or her work and help me adjust my vehicle's mirrors, nor did anyone begrudge me a Sharpie when I needed one. When I tried to give it back, they always told me to keep it. When I couldn't read the smudged address on a package, my T6 (the relief carrier) read the name, scratched his stubbly chin, and said, "Robert Low? Robert Low . . . That's 732 Twenty-eighth Street. Leave the package behind his potted plant." Most regular carriers had the hundreds of names and addresses on their route memorized. T6s, if they never took a regular route, knew the names of six routes by heart.

But help felt different when it came from young men. They lingered or stood slightly closer than needed. They beamed after showing me a shortcut or squeezed the backs of their necks after lifting a heavy package for me. Sometimes, they were more overt. "I'm so poor, buy me lunch," one said.

"I'm new—aren't you supposed to get *me* lunch?" I answered.

"How about I cook you dinner?"

An older lady carrier usually overheard and yelled, "Leave her alone! Get back to work!"

Another guy complained to anyone who would listen, "I wish I could win the lottery, so I could leave this godforsaken place and stop seeing all of you knuckleheads." Then he turned to me. "Except you. If I won the lottery, I'd ask you out."

The clerk with the long braid intervened. "Aw, man, I'm so jealous. What about me? You don't want to see me anymore?"

Another grandma scolded him. "Stop bothering her! Matter of fact, come here and help me put this in my hamper."

The meekest pickup lines were offered in the presence of loud, older women. But after leaving the station, I was alone for the rest of the day.

*   *   *

After Amazon Sunday, I picked up *pad see ew* and a Sprite, though I had given up soda years before. I thought I'd have to cook all my meals to compensate for the reduced wages, but no longer paying for drinks, movies, or shows made it easier to live on a budget. I ate at my kitchen island, walked Dolmangi, and upon my return was startled by the quantity of dirty take-out containers, as if someone else had eaten in my kitchen and left. The Zoom recording of the last grief group sat in my inbox. I tried to watch wholesome British cooking competitions, but I became antsy. I craved human company. Though I saw more people, at work, than the vast majority of quarantined people, I wanted to goof around, to hug someone. Patty and Minyoung had been asking to go on a walk, but I felt nervous about the risk of exposing them.

I thought of which of my co-workers I could imagine getting a beer with. None of the young men, and it'd be hard with someone whose English wasn't great. I settled on Ayesha. She was around my age, down to earth, and I liked her enormous styrofoam Safeway coffee cups. I was curious whether she grew up in the city, what her story was. But the thought of carefully wording my request to hang out so it didn't seem burdensome or desperate, then making sure we actually got along, required energy I didn't have. Instead, I wrote another letter to Esther—with whom I'd already done that work.

> Dear Esther,
> I had my first sexual thoughts since you died. I was driving to my route when I started playing a little game: Which sex act would suit each co-worker who hit on me? For the one that sneaks forlorn, wistful glances and accidentally blurted out "But I love her!" when someone accused him of throwing a package at my head—I would let him eat me out on a pallet at the station after everyone left. He looks like he'd enjoy the act of worship. For the miserable one who chugs Red Bulls, chain-smokes, complains, and comes by my case or my vehicle to ask

me to take some of his packages—I would drive out to his route and suck his dick in his truck. That would cheer/shut him up. Last, there's the one who is always showing me tricks for using the scanner, how to case the mail for large apartments, how to double-stack the bins for durability. I thought—I'd take him home to my apartment and make love to him on my bed (!). I was kind of surprised by that. Like, really? I wondered if I had a crush on him. I don't think so. Sex is weird.

This time, I pressed colorful stickers onto the envelope and wrote her name and address in skinny bubble letters, like she used to. I stuck on the stamp, crossed it out with a Sharpie, wrote *dec* on the front, and slipped it into my satchel.

8

"Why don't you want to come?" Esther's mouth hung open, and she was curling her eyelashes to a scary degree. They stood up straight like terrified spider legs.

I wiped my hands on the back of my jeans. The sink was begging me to clear it of its dirty dishes. Esther told me not to, but when I started, she let me. She had washed the dishes at my home growing up as well. Not because she cared about cleanliness but as a thank-you for the meals.

At eighteen, we'd both left the Los Angeles area for the Bay. Esther was at San Francisco State and I was at Stanford. Sometimes on weekends, I'd take Caltrain to visit her. We agreed San Francisco had more to see than Palo Alto. This time, she wanted me to accompany her to her boyfriend's show. A stoner-skater with unwashed long hair, potato chip crumbs on his shirt, and a sad smile, Tyler was a white male version of her, only wealthier and stupider. His mother calling her "Oriental" didn't stop Tyler and Esther from making out on the bus, in bars, at parties; they were in lust and didn't care who knew it. Neither Esther nor I had had any crushes in high school, only the occasional sexual tension with some boys in our classes. Since she played soccer and volleyball, Esther flirted with the boys on the respective teams, but her having a boyfriend—any boyfriend—was new for us. She told me he was "laid-back, funny, and sweet," and how once, after watching a Linklater movie with her, he looked "so high on life it was inspiring."

"I don't visit that often. Couldn't we do something just us?" Esther was the only person to whom I would make such bald requests. I usually endured silently.

"What are you down to do then?"

"I want to get drunk and go for a walk."

This was how we normally spent our evenings together, collapsing into the same bed at the end of the night, waking up to each other's dried, stinking breaths. I never felt bad about drinking, even if we were underage. I figured God understood better than anyone else that I had things I wanted to forget. I was hungover and reeking of vodka in the pews on Sunday mornings, and the people next to me needed to study the Bible verses on forgiveness and judge not lest ye be judged. Esther had no such hang-ups, though over the phone one time she admitted she'd "had a few slipups where I should have called it quits. Nothing too embarrassing, just silly drunk decisions I never would've made sober." For Esther this mostly meant the distinction between inside and outside disappeared, which resulted in her yelling or cheering at strangers or peeing in public. She continued, "It's like this line in Cat Power's 'Colors and the Kids': 'It's so hard to go into the city 'cause you wanna say, "Hey, I love you," to everybody.' One of those nights." Whereas drinking helped me forget things enough to relax, Esther carried her edginess, elation, or whatever she was feeling close to the surface. She didn't need alcohol to get rid of her inhibitions, it just turned her volume up. It was a trait of hers that I was jealous of and concerned about.

"We can drink at the show," Esther said.

"Then we don't have to stay after?"

She was quiet as she applied her tinted lip balm. Then she asked, "Have you liked anyone before?"

I sat on my hands. "I've thought some guys were hot, yeah."

"Does anything come out of it?"

My face warmed. "No."

"Because you don't want to? Or you're scared?"

"I don't want to." I said this with assurance. "I think guys can be beautiful, like a painting or sculpture. But I don't want to touch them."

"Have you ever wanted to date someone?"

"No." I figured in high school that teenagers were all lousy and that I'd find someone in college. Halfway through my sophomore year, no such person had appeared. My classmates weren't exactly lame, but their romantic overtures reminded me of the mating dances of jungle birds, fascinating and alien, intended for another audience. I began to pity anyone who asked me out, as if I'd inadvertently fooled him into thinking I was normal.

"So, you've never gotten pumped or nervous when someone called you?"

"Sometimes when I'm making a new friend. But for a guy, no."

She thought for a moment. Then she grabbed a pair of scissors from her desk drawer and pulled over a trash can. Sitting on the floor in front of the mirror, she thinned out her hair. "Do you like girls?"

I mentally scanned the various things I masturbated to—I'd masturbated since I was three years old—searching for a girl.

Amid all the prohibitions and limitations of my childhood, pleasuring myself—usually humping the arm of the couch while my mom was out or rubbing myself in the shower in the mornings—was one of the few things in life I could help myself to. No one ever told me it was a sin; the main issue with onanism was spilled seed. Onan was having sex with Tamar in the Bible; it wasn't masturbation.

"I don't think I like girls," I said. "Though I've felt hot and bothered around Patty before."

"Yeah, everyone has a crush on her. I feel sorriest for the straight guys. Would you date her?"

I considered. "No." The thought of pursuing or touching Patty in a romantic or sexual way did nothing for me. Or more precisely, it felt insincere. She didn't deserve that. There was also God's aversion to gayness in the Bible. I reasoned non-Christians didn't have to follow the rules because He wasn't their god (the same way they weren't obliged to tithe), and I'd never met a gay Christian, so the question wasn't personally urgent. Otherwise, my sexual purity was in the same category as my sobriety. Ideals, but less important. I assumed I would see why premarital sex was sinful when or if I ever experienced it firsthand.

"Do you *want* to like anyone?"

Esther cared enough to ask, was the only one allowed to ask. I knew nothing would make her leave me, and I needed her to tell me when I was being stupid. I likewise wanted to behold Esther in her entirety. I was curious about her sexuality but not enough to have sex with her. Which was something Tyler could give her. There was a glimpse of how our friendship could diminish or end.

"I can't tell if I want to or if I just want to fit in."

"I don't mean to make you feel self-conscious. It's cool if you don't." She stood up, rummaged through her desk, and handed me a pair of craft scissors. "Could you cut my bangs?"

I glanced askance at the zigzag edges of the scissors. "I don't want to fuck up your hair."

"Just try. Cut like this." She gestured with her fingers upward.

I positioned myself in front of her, both of us sitting cross-legged with our knees touching. Esther faced the mirror behind me. "I want to have a baby, though," I said as I held her bangs between the fingers of my left hand and held the scissors in my right.

"Now?"

"Not now. But if I got pregnant, would you help me take care of it?"

"Bitch, you better not get pregnant soon. But for sure."

For a few minutes, we said nothing. Dead Skeletons played in the background. I was snipping as little as I possibly could, and the dullness of the scissors, which often bent rather than cut her hair, made us laugh. We gave up, and she put the rest of her thick hair up in a high, bouncy ponytail.

"I would drop out of school to help you raise your baby, too," I said.

"Duh. But I don't want a kid."

"Ever?"

"I mean if it happens"—she shrugged—"but if it doesn't, that's cool, too. So, when you dress up to go out, are you ever trying to hook up with anyone?"

"I think I just like feeling pretty." I glanced at the mirror, skeptical. I was wearing a white halter top, skinny jeans, and knee-length suede boots. My long, straight hair covered my back pimples. My cheeks were still chubby, and even with kohl-lined eyes, I looked fourteen, like an underage sex worker. Esther's dressing up meant curled, mascaraed eyelashes, blush, tinted lip balm, and chandelier earrings, but otherwise, she wore what she'd wear to class or to work as a waitress—thick black eyeliner, a short, boxy blue corduroy skirt, a loose faded-blue tank top, long black cotton socks, and black Vans. She had an effortless French vibe, but she also looked like a high schooler.

"Hasn't anyone tried to kiss you?"

"None successfully." I remembered a humid dorm party during which a boy pulled my face up toward his, but I quickly clenched my jaws and bared my teeth and he ended up kissing my gums and incisors. I was not a sexy college student. I was not a floating yellow balloon of youth. Something heavier and more slippery.

"Are you grossed out by sex?"

"In my imagination it's good. In movies it looks good. But real life, the thought of touching someone is disgusting."

"What movies?" She was surprised I'd never seen any porn and pulled out her laptop, though I requested gay porn only.

"Why?"

"I want straight sex to be a surprise."

It was my first time seeing an erect penis. I'd never seen anything like it. The other man's mustachioed mouth seemed better suited than mine for sucking its enormousness. How would my smaller mouth ever manage? Watching the repeating up-and-down, in-and-out motion of the cock in the butthole was mesmerizing. All my years of masturbating had centered on fantasies of kissing, nudity, and caresses, but no penetration of any sort—in imagination and in practice. It had never crossed my mind, though I'd understood it on a theoretical level.

"There's feminist porn, too, but you usually have to pay."

"What?"

She waved her hand, "Ah, forget it."

I kept it in mind for future reference.

"I like physical intimacy. I miss it when I don't have it." She turned to me and shrugged. "But sex doesn't make you cool. Everyone's an idiot when they're having sex. Maybe try it out if you want to, but don't force it. That'd be like raping yourself with another body. You don't have shit to prove."

"Thanks. Do you think true love exists, and that I should wait for it?"

"Sex is better when you like each other. I think true love exists, but it's rare. You can't expect to find it so easy. But that's okay—sometimes you can have a connection with someone for just a few months or even a night. Though it's risky business because you can wake up the next morning like, 'Fuck, why did I do that?'" She laughed loudly.

"Because you realize you hate him?"

"What? No, like, he's lame, the sex wasn't good, or you get an STD and it wasn't worth it."

I took this in, then confessed, "So much of the world has no relevance to me. Romantic love and sex seem to be in that category. But it looks nice in movies, and so many people are obsessed with it. I wonder if I'm missing out."

"It's there if it's there. If not, there's something else." Esther didn't stress it. She smacked her tinted lips together. "Okay, we'll go to the show, stay for, like, five minutes, just so I can holler at Tyler and let him know how he did. Then we can go walk."

"Deal."

*　　*　　*

At the bar, the security guard kicked Esther out for being too drunk and bumping into too many people while dancing. I didn't think she was drunk. That was just Esther being into it. Grinning with her mouth open, rocking her body, nodding her head, stomping her feet—she was as exuberant as anyone I'd seen at a revival or retreat. I followed as the security guard escorted her out. We shared a smoke, but then she darted back in when he wasn't looking. After the band's set, I told Tyler, who played bass, that I enjoyed the show, and Esther and he kissed and shouted in each other's ears before Esther yanked me by my arm, and we ran out.

Instead of staying in the Mission where other revelers crowded the sidewalks, we decided to save $1.75 in ticket fare and walk an hour and a half home instead. Gradually, the young crowds, Mexican families, bacon-wrapped hot dogs, graffiti, neon signs, and buses that heaved when they knelt faded into Noe Valley's empty sidewalks, swaying willows, bottlebrush trees, and Victorian houses painted in hues that demonstrated the egos of their owners. Esther took us on a detour up Tank Hill. We stared at the thick fog blanketing the city lights, but we couldn't stay long because the wind was blowing something terrible. Sobered up, we stopped by a 7-Eleven to buy more cigarettes, Hot Cheetos, and frozen slushies, into which we emptied tiny bottles of vodka. The air was cool on my damp skin; the syrupy snow slid down my throat. I didn't have to think because Esther was the one who was guiding us—north to Golden Gate Park.

It was like walking together after school in Torrance, except we were drunk and smoking and the moon was close and bright. My stomach started to cramp to the point where it was hard to straighten my back, but I thought I could walk it off. I asked

Esther about sex, the pros and cons of the different positions, how transitions between positions worked.

I thought about the porn. "Have you tried anal?"

"Yeah, it's pretty cool. That's when I know he's my bitch."

Somewhere around the Panhandle, I told her my mother was begging my dad to consider using government-provided nurses for in-home care, but he didn't want to lose the income my mom received for doing it herself. When I was home from college, I was responsible for all the housework—cooking, cleaning, car registration and oil changes, Section 8 and food stamp paperwork, and sometimes helping my dad eat. My mom handled the sponge baths, the diaper changes, and the bills. She never hugged me or offered a kind word, but she did protect me from that. She wouldn't let me give up Stanford for a commuter college, but with me gone, she couldn't manage on her own. In preparation for my going away, she had taken beauty school classes in the evenings and knew someone who could rent her a chair at a hair salon. But my dad didn't want strangers wiping his ass. This was past his limit. My dad could only assert himself so much, so he stopped eating. A hunger strike.

My mom had vented to me over the phone, and I wondered if she was in the house where he could hear. The only words of comfort I knew she would receive were about the long suffering of Christ. His body bleeding on the cross, the weight of the world's sins on his shoulders, begging God to let the cup pass. We never suffered alone but entered into the suffering of Christ, receiving a small glimpse of what He did for us. And Jesus still walked out of the tomb three days later. God would never give us more than we could bear. Our family had no one else but God—I believed this last point especially. What human could touch my father's heart or truly understand his pain and humiliation? Only God could provide the supernatural strength, grace, and love that enabled us to be there for one another. And the church was there to remind us.

When speaking with my dad, he lied that he and my mother had come to an agreement. I pretended that this agreement would be in-home care, and I praised the benefits of nurses who'd cared for many people and knew how to keep a professional distance. But he changed the subject and asked how my studies were going. He told me to eat well, sleep well, and not overdo it, and to find a husband in college. *I waited too long. When I was becoming too old to marry, all that was left was your mother.*

Far away from home, at a school that provided all my meals and cleaning service in the dorms for free, I felt a combination of relief and guilt—and bitterness about my guilt. I downed the rest of my slushy cup in one large gulp.

Esther wrapped her arm around my shoulders. "Family are the people who've done more for you than anyone else, hurt you more than anyone else, and ask for more than anyone else. That's why you wish you could give them everything and run away from them at the same time."

"And friends?"

"Eh, friends can become family."

"We're family?" Maybe because Esther had so many more people she called family, it was easier for her to include people into the term. *Family* was such a fraught term for me, I didn't know if I wanted to embroil Esther into it.

"You're in my life forever now. If you ever ran away from me, I wouldn't accept it. I'd hunt you down."

"So you don't want to run away from me?"

"No, we chose each other. Nothing we do for each other is weighed down by guilt or blood. It feels lighter."

"Wouldn't considering me family make it heavier?"

Esther shrugged. "For some reason it doesn't."

I put my arm through hers, holding my empty cup and unfinished chips, the fabric of her jean jacket stiff against me. I told her she could help her family in other ways. Now it wasn't just my stomach, but something lower in my intestines seizing up and sending alarms to my brain. I flexed, rubbed her back, patted her shoulders. We took turns lighting each other's cigarettes though I couldn't finish mine. Esther told me that her own family wasn't doing much better. Her parents had opened credit cards using her oldest brother's Social Security number and then defaulted on their payments. At twenty-seven, her brother couldn't rent an apartment or take out a loan. Her brothers pitched in to help pay off the debt, but Esther had stayed uninvolved, which had stirred up resentment. They had covered so much of her tuition that they thought she could spare some of her waitressing income. Esther thought her parents needed to downsize—get rid of the luxury rental car, sell the house, and move somewhere cheaper. Esther's mother and one of her brothers agreed, but her father and other two brothers didn't.

As she spoke, I quietly prayed to God from the center of my being to the center of His being, advocating for Esther, pleading for help, fortitude, and perspective for Esther and her family.

"My family's a sinking ship," she said. "But if I stay out of it, after everything they've done for me, I look like a spoiled brat."

"You're not a spoiled brat. You call and text your parents and brothers from your busted-ass phone, and you think about them so much. They're stressed and saying things they don't mean. You're in college. What can you do? When things settle down, they'll be relieved you didn't get involved."

We stumbled into a Walgreens to use the bathroom, where the fluorescent light stabbed our eyes and made the entire store look ugly. In the bathroom, I locked the door behind us, and Esther headed toward the toilet first.

"Esther don't—" The seat was up and on the rim were a mix of drops and stains, but it was too late.

"Whatever, I don't care." She truly didn't.

I looked away into the mirror, my face sweaty and my eye makeup smudged all around. I bent my knees a little to relieve the violent churning in my stomach and the urgent pressure pushing against my rectum. I clenched as hard as I could and waited for Esther to finish.

"What should I do about my brothers?"

"What is there left to do?" I heard the toilet paper roll spooling off and counted down the seconds.

"I could take a trip down to visit." The toilet flushed.

I rushed over, slammed down the seat, wiped it with toilet paper. I warned Esther, "You can leave, I'm going number two." But just as Esther was about to open the door, the smell and sound of my watery diarrhea spewing into the bowl filled the room. Esther had no choice but to close the door and wait for me to finish.

"I'm sorry," I said, mortified.

"Oh my God! Miriam!" She crumpled into a squat with her hands still on the doorknob and cackled. "It smells fucking awful!" Her laughter sounded like crying, and it echoed against the walls.

I couldn't join in her hyena yips because I was in too much pain. I was sweating from nausea as well. This, too, was a type of intimacy.

9

Mondays were the worst because every address received a thin paper booklet of local store ads. This was known as Marriage Mail since it was "married" to every address. All carriers knew that Marriage Mail—which intensified every step of casing, loading, and delivery and beat up our bodies—was trash. That Marriage Mail went straight to recycling. Our weekly sand mandala. And not just Marriage Mail: most of the mail we delivered was trash. Occasionally there were kernels of worth, such as paychecks or car registration stickers, but honestly, even without the Marriage Mail, we spent most our days delivering garbage.

As Esther had asked, What was it all for? The way Joanne's knees were completely fucked? Ernie's son studying mechanical engineering at UC Davis? The Tesla I saw Resy drive up in? I knew the pay steadily increased with seniority, but how much did Resy work to afford a Tesla?

On Monday, I was the last carrier out of the station because I took forever to integrate my Marriage Mail with my flats and hot case. Ayesha didn't integrate her Marriage Mail and instead kept it in the separate bundles. She took three days to deliver it.

"Like any customer's going to notice their Marriage Mail is late," she said.

Out in the parking lot, carriers were loading their vehicles, moving their hampers to and from the station. At her vehicle, Ayesha shouted out to the rest of us as she organized her packages. "C'mon, everybody, let's say it together: I . . . hate . . . my . . . job!"

Everyone within earshot laughed.

She repeated, "Let me hear you! I . . . hate . . . my . . . job! I . . . hate . . . my . . . job!"

The sun was shining, and the sky was blue.

I remembered I'd been taught "Whatever you do, work heartily, as for the Lord and not for men." All work—from toilet scrubbing to child-rearing to leading a company—was an act of worship. Work was sanctified by God, measured by standards of love and truth. We had a heavenly audience whose ideals of perfection were complete and understood to be unattainable for humans. Sanctifying work contained a desire to transcend the material and mundane by digging deeper into the material and mundane. It was not about human recognition.

Though maybe it was a ploy to create low-paid, productive workers who didn't revolt—the "opiate for the masses."

Why did it seem that messages of humility and service failed to penetrate the ones who needed to hear them while the downtrodden heard little else? I thought of how working-class Korean churches had more sermons about forbearance, long-suffering, reward in the afterlife, and testimonies of miraculous deliverance and healing, whereas churches around Stanford and the upper-middle-class church I'd gone to in San Francisco preached about how believing that Christ died for our sins came before anything we did. Salvation by faith, not by works. Did software engineers need to hear their freedom from damnation came at the cost of someone else's suffering? Even within each of the churches, the women, the undocumented, the ones from poorer backgrounds wrestled with "serving and forgiving others as Christ served and forgave you." What if Stanford students and upper-middle-class San Franciscans listened to the sermons of long-suffering preached-to Korean immigrants? If Korean immigrants were told they were "more than conquerors" with nothing to be ashamed of?

I was also taught that work existed before the Fall, in the Garden of Eden. Labor in paradise. Even God worked—after creating the universe, he rested on the seventh day. Adam gardened and named the animals, though, importantly, Eden watered itself. This implied that work was inherently good, but survival didn't depend on it. Humans had time to walk with God, naked and unashamed. Only after the Fall was work cursed with thorns, thistles, and the sweat of one's brow. Work was corrupted, top to bottom, but still, we were to work for the Lord.

Some people wanted to re-create Eden—a life without hard labor, only the kind that was fun to do, like naming animals and leisure gardening. But every human life required backbreaking, dirty work: the labor of growing and manufacturing food, procuring drinking water, clearing waste, building and sustaining infrastructure, transporting goods, caring for the sick, the elderly, and the very young. That's why it was called essential—the government had come up with the right word for it. But instead of its ensuring well-being, dignity, and gratitude for anyone who did the dirty work, our aspiration was to never do it and to never be reminded that others did it for us. We dreamed of hogging all the rest. Though sometimes I fantasized about sanitation workers and migrant farmers vacationing in luxurious mountain resorts and on tropical beaches where they were gently fed and massaged into bliss.

Even fallen work had its Edenic moments. When certain mailboxes were accessible yet secure. My happiest moments were on rare light days, when I could easily carry mail for both sides of the street in my left hand and arm, the satchel barely filled. The lack of strain as I flew by several houses in a row with no mail for them I experienced as a deep physical happiness.

Every day, with each address, each release, the weight in my arms, hands, and shoulders got lighter. At one end of the block, for a moment, my hands and arms were gorgeously empty. Then I reached into my satchel and took out the other side of the street's mail. As I made my way back to my truck, I released mail little by little. By the end, my empty satchel flopped loosely.

No matter how tightly packed the vehicle was in the morning, somehow, at the end of the day, there was nothing left.

* * *

Everyone drove off to their routes, and I was alone in the station, heaving my overweight mail and flats into my hamper because of all the Marriage Mail. The entire building was empty, and I felt like an idiot. I remembered my trainer at the Carrier Academy: "No matter how frustrated you are with the mail, do *not* dump it in the trash. Throwing away someone else's mail is a federal crime. You *will* go to jail, I repeat, you *will* go to jail." The PowerPoint slide had a photo of Marriage Mail, a trash bin crossed out with red lines, and a stock image of a person crying behind bars.

On the street, there was nothing like constant, low-grade suffering to hold the mind in the moment, fill the present and expand it. I couldn't have too many thoughts while delivering mail because looking at the last two digits of the addresses, my mind sounded like this: *02, 02, 02, 02, 04, 06, 06, 10, 10, 10, 10, 12, 12, 12, 16, 20, 20, 20, 20, 20, 20, 20, 22, 22* . . . Even when my arms were empty, I was thinking of the next block, the next side street. On Mondays, I had to stop by every single mailbox.

Delivering mail helped me not to think about death. How did humans not obsess about it all the time? People in lockdown didn't understand. All their whining on social media grated on me. The silence of the empty streets felt more appropriate. Job said, "I put my hand over my mouth." What were the sounds in the hospital?

As I fingered the envelopes and read the addresses, I couldn't think about how the city refused to show Esther's family the footage from Van Ness station's security cameras for fear it would be too painful. I knew a church acquaintance, a civil engineer for Muni, who had access to the tapes, and he described it to me. The angle of the camera didn't show the ledge that Esther fell from, but it showed her landing feetfirst onto the tracks. The ledge was about two stories high. Muni stopped the trains after her fall, but her body lay there for hours, unattended. Without the need to find each apartment's mailbox or mail opening, I would have turned it over like a bitter lozenge in my mouth, whether her dying happened in an instant or over hours.

Back in the truck, I took a sip of water and thought about my mother telling me about *gaeksa*, the Korean word for dying outside one's home. The distinct tragedy of dying unaccompanied and unknown. Though in fraught conditions, my father had at least died in his bed, with the privacy to cover his indignity. Esther's corpse had lain exposed, a public spectacle.

I mulled over how Esther hadn't seem depressed to me. Quite the contrary, she'd seemed upbeat, making plans for graduate school to become a special education teacher. She'd started drinking again, but it seemed more under control. There was the possibility of drugs the night she died. Minyoung guessed this when Esther came to her dance class, but wasn't sure.

I remembered another Korean saying, which Esther's mom said: *"A child that leaves before her parents is a bitch."* She was clearly paraphrasing.

I had also yelled at Esther in my head. *How could you leave me like this?*

I crouched in the back of the truck and tossed the next block's packages to the front. I organized the packages in order and drove to the next street. I filled my empty satchel with the next street's mail.

33, 33, 33, 35, 35, 41A, 41A, 41A, 41A, 41B, 47, 47, 47, 47, 47, 47, 47, 47, 47, 47, 47, 47, 47, 47, 47, 47, 47 . . . The house 747 Thirtieth Avenue received the thickest handful of mail each day—political ads with Black or brown politicians' faces leering and sneering on the envelopes, threatening to bring sharia law or to unleash criminals onto the streets. Except one with Ben Carson's angelic face: "Democrats want to bring back Jim Crow, but nothing will stop me from expressing my faith."

* * *

With only thirty minutes left for me to deliver, my vehicle was still half-full. Once the flats and the Marriage Mail were integrated, they needed to be delivered on the same day or the next day's flats would be completely mucked. I didn't want to stay out so late, and I wasn't sure if I was even allowed to. As with every question, I texted Resy.

She told me to text my location and situation to our supervisor, Jyothi. Then, *Your Achilles' heel! Finally, you're acting like a brand-new carrier.* I could almost hear Resy's chipmunk giggle.

Next thing I knew, two co-workers cinematically drove up to me, speeding around the corner with their side doors open and no seat belts on, almost falling out of their vehicles. Their hard faces made them look like public-servant cowboys. They were breaking the safety rules to deliver more quickly because no one had time to shut those doors or put on seat belts when we were constantly getting in and out of the vehicle. They loaded the bulk of my packages and mail into their empty trucks, which filled me with embarrassment and gratitude. The shame I felt for creating extra work for them comingled with my awe at how quickly they prepped and delivered Marriage Mail, with extra time to deliver mine. Both of them finished and returned to the station before I did.

MM is hard for everyone in the beginning, Resy reassured me via text.

*   *   *

At home, Dolmangi whined loudly when I saw him through my window to the backyard. My heart broke, and I gave him extra treats and kisses after he bolted in through the door. I fed him dinner, walked him quickly around the block, and filled my own plate with a grown-man-size portion of Japanese curry with rice. After finishing it, I was as hungry as before. So I ate another heap of curry rice, then a bag of plantain chips, and five lemon sandwich cookies. I'd been shedding pounds, as all carriers did when they started. Resy said the drastic weight loss was the real reason for the ninety-day probation before giving new carriers uniform allowance. That and the turnover rate.

Thinking about the uniform immediately perked my spirits. I already knew which one I wanted. On the USPS employee website, I eyed the less popular but undeniably cute dark navy, A-line, knee-length skirt. I'd wear it with the baby-blue collared shirt with red, navy, and white pinstripes. In the winter, I'd wear a simple long-sleeve and the midnight-blue sweater vest with red piping and embroidered white eagle. I didn't know what my budget was, but these were on my wish list. I had already found an unused visor with a fantastically wide brim in my vehicle. Resy said I could keep it. I drew pictures of the uniform I wanted on a letter to Esther. Then I took out my color pencils.

*   *   *

When I woke up in the morning, my body ached all over. Resy told me her own body took two months to get used to the job and that 80 percent of new hires quit during the first two months. The most surprising pains were in my fingers and the sides of my hands. She promised it would get better. The soreness made me wonder if this job was a bad idea since I had a college degree, but this was what I felt capable of. Plus, there was health insurance and retirement.

The mail still had to be delivered. Thankfully, after my body warmed up, the aches and pains slowly disappeared. I decided to start stretching before I slept.

*   *   *

Ayesha held her styrofoam cup of coffee in one hand and a small cooler in the other. She poked her head into my case.

"You finished all your Marriage Mail?" she said.

"Yeah, but two people had to come help me."

Stacks of untouched Marriage Mail sat in her case. Technically, integrating the flats was against the rules. Ayesha hadn't delivered it all on time, but she was only following instructions. It was something Manwai, who purposefully followed the rules so as to deliver slowly, would have approved of. And based on Ayesha's uniform, she had finished probation, so her job was secure.

"I heard you've started delivering a full route, too," she said with a sigh.

"Is that bad?"

"And you cased your own mail on your first day."

I felt like I was in trouble.

Ayesha put her coffee down. "Let me tell you something. I'm only saying this because I have some friends who are carriers who've been doing this for a while. They told me that the sooner you deliver a full route on time, the sooner they'll give you overtime. And not just once or twice a week, but all six days of the week, ten-, twelve-hour days. And you'll have to do it because you're still on probation, *and* you're still PTF. You'll have no life. Second of all, you're making me look bad." She grinned.

"Oh, sorry! I didn't know."

"I'm kidding. But I'm for real about not running your route. It's not good for you. The supervisor's going to take advantage of you."

I appreciated her concern, but the postal service could run me into the ground for all I cared. Slowing down was detrimental to my emotional well-being. I said, "Okay, thanks," trying to end the conversation. If Ayesha and I came back to the station at different times, she didn't have to know when I finished. Though how did she know all that information to begin with?

"And another thing," she added. "People get irritated if you run your route."

"How come?"

"It ruins the route when there's an adjustment. They track you with the GPS in your scanner. If you deliver too fast, they make the route longer. Route ten is a good route. Don't mess it up. You're not going to be on it long anyways. Take all your breaks."

"Thanks."

Ayesha went to get her hamper, and I went to grab the keys to my vehicle. Passing by her case, I noticed a photograph hanging at the top. A cute baby wearing a dinosaur onesie, strapped into a car seat, staring at me with such skepticism. The almond-shaped eyes that looked exactly like Ayesha's. I held my breath. Babies were such small, inscrutable beings. Christ came as a baby. The Savior of the world in diapers. I was surprised Esther's death hadn't changed how moved I felt around new life.

And I saw why Ayesha didn't prioritize finishing her Marriage Mail on time. She wouldn't be able to go drinking with me anyway; she had a baby. Lucky her.

*   *   *

At home, it was more Japanese curry. I'd made a huge pot for the week. I answered an email from the long-term substitute teacher about the password for the teacher's iPad, and how to use the projector for the PowerPoint. I saw that my students were learning about the ethics of mercy over justice. I read emails from old church friends asking how I was, asking if I wanted to Zoom or catch up with a walk on the beach. I didn't want to ignore their kindness and concern, but what did we have in common now that I didn't love Jesus? None were friends I would have chosen. God had chosen them for me, but God and I weren't talking anymore.

My mother called, which was odd. I usually initiated. *"What's your address?"*

I told her. She wanted to send me some face masks. She had also started making her own kimchi—a first. People weren't getting their hair cut or dyed, so she was living off a small-business loan to keep her afloat.

She asked if I had heard of dating apps. Someone at church said her son met his wife on Coffee Meets Bagel, an app invented by two Korean women, so it must be trustworthy.

"Omma, it's the pandemic. *I can't go on dates."*

"What about the park? It's safe outside, six feet apart. I met with a young deacon at the park. He helped me set up Zoom on my phone so I could watch the church services. You can't lock yourself in just because Esther died. She wouldn't want that either."

"No one is dating right now, Omma. You either have a partner or you don't. And I don't like those apps."

"Why?"

"Just." I couldn't explain to her the torture of creating a dating profile. I lauded the ones who found their soulmates online, but the apps were not for me.

"You want to live alone your whole life?"

I looked at framed photographs on the wall—church friends at a retreat, Patty, Minyoung, me with Esther by a lake, and me with Esther at our high school graduation bowling night. I said, *"You enjoy living alone more than you enjoyed being married."*

"What happened to me was an extremely rare tragedy. It's better to be with a good person than alone. And it's better to be alone than with . . . a difficult person."

I dug my nails into my arm. *"Please leave my dead father alone."*

"You should have met someone while you were at Stanford."

"My Stanford degree allows me to support myself. I'm fine." Now would not be the time to tell her I was delivering mail, and that my co-workers were immigrants, some around her age. My mother assumed I was teaching Scripture online, and I didn't correct her. Even though it had been years since she hit me, I was afraid she would drive all the way up to San Francisco and beat the shit out of me.

After hanging up, I thought about my dad. When they got married, he had a black belt in tae kwon do and carried her with ease. He was always soft-spoken, but I couldn't tell if it was his lack of energy and depression.

Before he died, I did all I could to show my respect and regrets, but I never got to know the extent of the abuses he endured when I wasn't home. I didn't know how to ask. Now I had no way to comfort him. I used to believe God comforted him after death, had imagined my dad in the blissful peace of God's presence with no boundary between them, but now, I had to grapple with both of them potentially not existing in any spiritual form.

I wished I could still believe in resurrection. What I would do to hug Esther again, to see my father in an exalted state! The loss of belief in life after death was a deep ache, but I couldn't go back. I no longer knew how anyone could be sure of what happened after death.

At once, my sadness and loneliness became unbearable. I wrung my hands, then held myself as I cried. I thought of how a celebrity pastor preached, "Don't waste your cancer"—meaning, use every tragedy to get closer to God. Confront mortality, cherish Jesus, glorify God with praise and trust. It rang true when I felt myself to be in a dark, dank pit, and I delighted in God's cosmic joy as "while Joseph was there in prison, the LORD was with him." Even with clenched teeth, every difficult moment would become a memory of intimacy with God. At my breakfast nook in the fading light, where was He now?

I looked down. Dolmangi was asleep at my feet on the floor of the kitchen, his curly tail wound around the leg of my chair, the rise and fall of his belly light but steady. We shared a home, but he only lived in the present and his immediate, material reality. He didn't seem to know anything about the pandemic, Esther's death, or hell. His emotions centered on the joy of walking, eating, and pets, the pain of loneliness, the thrill of chasing prey and sniffing scents, the torture of baths, and the fear of thunder, fireworks, and the vacuum cleaner. In between everything were naps, occasional vomiting from eating too quickly, or ripping open a treat bag I accidentally left within his reach. His world within my world was a small, warm room off to the side.

In a burst of selfishness, I got down onto the floor and threw my arms and chest over him, covering his warm, furry body like a blanket. He startled, craned his neck, and searched my face, then plopped back down, resigning himself to be smothered. Esther loved her dog, Maggie, so much she would run to pet any beagle she saw in the street crying, "Maggie!"—ignoring the owner completely. While others graffitied their names in bathroom stalls, Esther had always written *I miss my dog* with a drawing of Maggie's profile. I lay there on top of Dolmangi, stroking his velvet ears. He squirmed and stretched, then accepted his lot again.

The old me would have pitied the new me for seeking solace in a dog instead of God, the creature instead of the Creator. My past self would have felt frustrated, scared, and sorry for me, and my present self cringed at, hated, and felt disgusted by my past self. I was fragmented and unstable, taking what comfort I could from Dolmangi regardless of what the old me thought. I used to wonder how people lived every day without God. Now I knew. I was doing it. I tried to imagine what it would look like for my various selves to love each other. I couldn't.

I got up feeling slightly better, but the stone weight in my chest persisted. I wrote Esther another letter, wanting to talk about something completely different. To be with her somewhere else.

Esther,

I remember my mail lady always talked on the phone through her headphones while delivering mail. Other carriers listen to music, the radio, or comedians' sets. They could all do their routes backward with their eyes closed. Not me. I have to pay attention to every step.

You wouldn't believe how beat-up my feet are. Swollen, blisters, corns, and athlete's foot. My $160 Hokas are too small now, but Resy told me about Big 5's "delivery worker shoes" for $35. They are the bomb! So much space for my toes, which are now covered in a hard leather shell so I can bump them into anything. Really good ankle support, great for uneven sidewalks. It straight up feels palatial inside my shoes. My toes are all :-O "Wow! Omg look at all this space! Where's the bathroom?????"

You kept up your long walks all over the city after I became too lazy to go with you. You had an athlete's body with a little beer belly even though you stopped playing sports. You wore black leather clogs, Vans, or Adidas Sambas. You re-wore old socks if you didn't have clean ones. You offered to buy me more of the cute socks on sale at Gross Out, but when they were sold out, you washed half of your worn pack and gave them to me. I can still hear you say, "I got you, girl!"

I thought of you when I learned why all the address stickers on magazines are upside down, on the bottom left corner. Mail carriers hold magazines upside-down and grab them by the binding, which is an easier grip than the loose pages. I thought you'd enjoy the ubiquitous, unnoticed detail, the explanation behind it. Nothing in this world makes sense, least of all your absence. But here was one thing that did.

I miss you still.

10

Clerks started their days at one A.M., rolling pallets of packages into the middle of the circle of hampers and cages (metal containers about six feet tall). They scanned each parcel and threw it into the correct hamper/cage, and they organized the hot cases by route for carriers to pick up. This meant they had memorized every block in our zip code and to which of the thirty routes it belonged. A muscular carrier joined our clerk at five A.M., throwing packages alongside her as his overtime. By the time we trickled in, packages and parcels were flying all around the middle. When someone almost got hit in the head, they'd shout, "Forty-six days!" (the time off after getting injured on the job).

The clerk called to me when I was pushing my tall metal cage filled with packages.

"Yes?" I stopped moving. The rattling of the wheels was so loud, I had to stop to hear.

"Don't push. Pull. Watch." She walked in front of the cage, pulling it behind her.

I had broken a sweat pushing my wiggling cage with all my might. Pulling it made it glide and easier to steer. How much energy had I been wasting? My brow felt cool as I dragged it behind me, less hindered. Resy had shown me from where to push the hampers to ensure smoother movement and control— from the side that read PUSH FROM THE OTHER SIDE. I winced at my old habit of trying to find spiritual meaning in everything. Instead, I turned and shouted, "Thank you!"

"Are they bringing in more pallets?" I heard the clerk mutter as she stepped away. There was a faint beeping from the back entrance, where the big rigs pulled in.

It was mid-April, and the packages didn't end. By ten A.M., everyone should have left to deliver, but at eleven A.M., the clerk was still rolling in towers of boxes.

"People must be ordering more packages," a co-worker muttered.

All the jokes and laughter stopped. Everyone's face turned motionless and gray as the carriers eyed their watches. My vehicle was already full—how was I going to fit in another hamper? When I asked Resy for help, she didn't seem to mind taking a break to show me hidden crevices—behind the driver's seat, on the steps, under the platform. Mail carriers waited in their cases as the clerk threw more packages. Others pitched in and helped.

By the time I left the station, the sun was at its highest point.

* * *

Out on the streets, I checked my watch to see how behind I was—on my first street when I should have been halfway through. In front of me, two women were sitting on their front steps, wearing sweatpants, drinking wine, and complaining about how time meant nothing to them now due to the quarantine.

I imagined slapping their mail across their faces, shattering their wineglasses on the sidewalk. Instead, I handed them their mail, averting my eyes, feeling my sweat squish between my toes. That should have been Esther and me.

In the neighborhoods, appreciative signs had sprung up here and there. Messages in children's handwriting in colorful crayon: THANK YOU DELIVERY WORKERS or WE <3 ESSENTIAL WORKERS. Other messages thanked nurses, doctors, and first responders. My favorite hand-drawn poster was the one that said PLEASE LEAVE PACKAGES BY THE GARAGE because it meant I didn't have to climb up the stairs to the front door.

Patty and Minyoung had been texting and asking if I was safe delivering during the pandemic. I was glad the shelter-in-place gave me an excuse to avoid them, though I promised to FaceTime them soon. I could hear Esther's voice chastising me, but ventriloquizing her voice in my head made me sick. I also got more emails from church people. One of them mourned my loss and my absence in the community and admitted that she wrestled with the same theological questions that drove me insane. She asked if I wanted to talk on the phone. I remembered volunteering alongside her in Children's Ministry. I sent my regrets, saying delivering mail gave me no extra time.

It was another way my job was saving me. My one day off per week was filled with grocery shopping, laundry, cleaning the house, and meal prep. On workdays, I walked Dolmangi at five thirty A.M. and was in bed by nine thirty P.M. I had just enough time after work to shower, eat dinner, feed and walk Dolmangi, and do my stretches before bed. My mechanical focus on completing a list of tasks continued at home, and for that I was grateful. But tonight, with such a late start, I wouldn't have time for my evening routine. Something would have to be compromised.

*   *   *

I returned to the station at eight P.M., stunned, listless, and famished. By Jyothi's desk, I heard Resy shouting, something about how those "damn assholes can't do this to us." I heard the authority in her voice. I remembered how some carriers called her *shifu*, or master teacher. Resy also broke rules other carriers were too scared to break (e.g., delivering mail without a satchel or dog spray).

It was dark outside the station, but carriers congregated around the long line of pallets to be delivered the next day. "It's almost Christmas levels," someone behind me muttered.

"Like seeing snow in July," said another.

On the drive home, I absentmindedly hummed a melody until I remembered the lyrics: "Whom shall I fear? I know who goes before me, I know who stands behind, the God of angel armies is always by my side." It was a stress song.

Did God miss my voice singing to him? Did He notice it was even gone? Maybe I was a better friend to Esther than God was to me. If God existed, I didn't know if I liked Him.

When I got home, I felt guilty about how late I was feeding and walking Dolmangi. He never sulked or got mad at me: it was instant forgiveness and joy when he laid eyes on me. But if packages continued at this rate, Dolmangi would be left alone in the backyard for over twelve hours. I didn't know what to do.

The next morning Resy approached me. "I'm sorry you had to see that yesterday. I hate using bad words in front of younger carriers. I just didn't think they should have made us finish delivering everything yesterday."

"I heard nothing," I said. Then: "Is this really what Christmas is like?" My hands throbbed with pain, and my legs were stiff.

"We have extra helpers on Christmas instead of four carriers on vacation." She shook her head. "They don't usually treat us like this, so don't worry. Just keep up your good work. You won't get sent to another station."

Extra helpers on Christmas—elves? Sent to another station?

Resy told me some carriers had divided their homes in half to separate themselves from their elderly parents. Others continued wearing masks at home except in their own room and separate bathroom, taking their meals in their bedrooms. I resolved to avoid my co-workers more than before. I wasn't ready for Christmas in April.

II

Esther and I had miscommunicated about which Megabus we were taking down together for winter break our senior year of college, so I switched tickets and arrived home a day earlier than I had told my mother. She didn't hear me when I entered the apartment. Maybe she didn't care. I could hear her muffled shouting: *"How many times did I tell you not to do this shit!"* When I opened my parents' bedroom door, it smelled like vomit. My mom held my dad by his shirt and was violently slapping his face with her other hand. Without thinking, I yanked her by her hair. She slammed her knuckles into the side of my head, and I fell to the ground. I saw stars. I had no idea she was so strong. She stepped around me and exited the apartment.

When I came to, my dad was still lying on the bed, eyes swollen shut, breathing heavily. The left side of his face was bright red with torn skin.

Can you please come over? My mom hurt my dad, I texted Esther. She helped me clean the barf, the spilled porridge. We sat in silence. There was no one else I could tell.

When my mother returned a few days later, I was no longer able to look her in the face. She didn't say where she'd been, and I didn't ask. But her neck, shoulders, and hips were startlingly thin, her right hand bruised yellow and purple. My pity overwhelmed my fear until my fear overcame my pity. Where had she slept? How scared my father must have been, how degraded! How trapped we all were. I didn't want to be alone with them nor leave her alone with him. Esther visited as much as she could, sometimes staying at my place while I took a walk to get some air. My prayers to God were wordless. When I brought myself before His presence, all I could do was weep. God was the place where there was no pretending, the place that needed no explanation.

I worried Esther's family was mad at me for taking so much of her time during her Christmas break, but I was desperate to keep her. She arrived matter-of-factly every morning with a thermos and Maggie on a leash. She set down her backpack and took her shoes off by the door. We'd settle in the living room, and I'd cook us instant noodles or fry an egg on toast or we'd take out the *banchan* her mother had made. This time, there was no drama in her family, only the usual misery between her parents. She and her brothers played Pusoy and hadn't laughed that hard in ages. I didn't want to discuss my parents; I only wanted her company. She was family but not. We passed the time watching and rating commencement speeches on YouTube by various celebrities. We painted with the watercolors I had given her for her birthday. I chose the telephone-pole wires and clouds outside my window. She did my dusty television set with the tangle of wires underneath the stand. Then the pomegranate tree in her backyard.

"Does this leaf look corny?" she asked. After a long pause, she mumbled, "When in doubt, layer."

A couple of weeks later, she invited my family to her family's Christmas dinner.

Esther's brothers, sister-in-law, and sister-in-law's parents were there, as were her mother's cousin, his wife, and their two daughters. The older generation, including my mom and my dad in his wheelchair with a bandage on his face, sat at the dining table. We young people sat in the living room with plates on our laps. There were glass noodles, braised short ribs, marinated spinach, spicy bellflower roots, zucchini pancakes, fish pancakes, purple rice. I brought a Korean herb salad garnished with flying-fish roe, imitation crab, and a sesame dressing. Esther picked up giant pools of pumpkin pies from Costco. It all tasted like sand to me.

My parents were actors that night—even smiling or laughing at times. My dad joked about his mandatory military service in Korea. My mother proselytized as usual.

"I don't need to go to church," Esther's dad answered. *"They're just trying to take my money. I'm sure Miriam's mom isn't one of them, but there are so many hypocrites in those churches."*

My mom was quiet after that.

I felt like a puppet, someone else's voice coming out of my mouth, invisible strings pulling my hands. Perhaps that was what my parents felt, too. Our ordinary behavior troubled me as much as our violence did. But I knew this was better than spending Christmas alone with them at home.

I looked across the coffee table where Esther was sitting on the floor. She smiled at me with a smile I remembered often after her death—closemouthed, tired, lowered lids, eyes full of a tenderness exaggerated by the wine. She, too, seemed far away.

I spent the rest of my break trying to arrange a new in-home caretaker for my father. Medi-Cal office recordings advised calling after January 3. I left multiple voicemails with different social workers, filled out the paperwork, and paper-clipped IDs, bank statements, and Social Security cards. I told my dad to wait a little longer and bought him his favorite flavors of Ensure and a green crazy straw to drink it with. On New Year's Eve, I bought cow bones, rice cakes, and dumpling ingredients. We usually bought the New Year soup from a restaurant to go, but I wanted to cook my feelings out, channel my distress into a perfect bowl of soup. I replaced the boiling water until the bones emptied their marrows into the broth and emerged hollow. When I sat down to pleat the dumplings, my mom quietly sat next to me to help. The swelling on her hand had gone down, though the discoloration was still there. I prepared the thinly sliced threads of fried egg white and egg yolks, thin slices of roasted seaweed, and thin slices of scallions. I was asleep by ten but woke up to Esther's calls to have champagne with her at midnight. We watched fireworks from the parking lot of Stoner Park, passing a bottle back and forth, listening to Strange Boys on her iPod, one headphone each.

"Something good better happen in 2008," Esther said.

"We're graduating."

"Thank God. Well, I have to take summer school, but then I'll be free."

In the morning, I bowed to my dad, slowly kneeling down until I rested my forehead on the bedroom floor. It was a sign of devotion and respect. A bit of an apology as well. I wished him many blessings for the New Year. Then I sat on my knees as he gave me advice: *Don't study too hard. As long as you're happy and healthy, I'm fine. I'm so proud of you.* I hadn't done this since I was a kid when my grandparents were alive. I didn't like how it felt like a goodbye and had to stop myself from crying,

It was hard to request anything from my mom, but I timidly asked if she would like to receive my bow. She demurred as expected, so we ate my soup. I cooked and arranged the garnishes on the rice cakes and dumplings in the bone-broth soup and texted Esther a picture from my flip phone. She responded with a picture of her family's own rice cake soup.

As I enjoyed the warm, comforting bone broth, soft rice cakes, and soft dumplings with bursts of flavor, I watched how slowly my mom ate, which *banchan* she savored—the *kkakdugi*. By the bottom of the bowl, both of our faces were blushing and damp from the heat of the soup, and we sat back in repose. My mom wordlessly cleaned up everything afterward while I went to my dad's room and helped him eat his smaller portion, with the rice cakes and dumplings cut into small pieces, supplemented by Ensure.

Before I left, she pressed two folded $100 bills into my hand. We didn't discuss our desires or grievances, say I love you, I forgive you, or I'm sorry. This was what we managed. These were the familiar channels that allowed us to maintain connection, the shape of family. We avoided burdening each other by crying and soothed ourselves on our own, in private. We were lonely but together.

*   *   *

I was back at school when my mother called to tell me that my dad had died, before my request for a new caregiver had been processed. I didn't know whether to be reassured or unsettled when she added, *"The first thing the EMT and social workers checked was for signs of abuse. Don't worry. They found nothing."*

Was that contempt in her voice? Was she bragging that she killed him without getting caught? A wave of cold seeped into me. She didn't sound like she had been crying. Had my mother done other things to my father in my absence, or had I caught her in a singular moment? I couldn't ask directly. She was recently widowed. I was half-orphaned. Of my two parents, I was left alone with the flinty, hard one.

"I had to keep shutting his eyes after he died, while I waited for the EMT to arrive. His eyes kept opening, so I pushed them closed with my fingers again and again. I heard they could harden like that and stay permanently open."

* * *

"I'm glad you have your faith," Esther said when the funeral was over and we were smoking outside a Korean buffet in Los Angeles. "It seems helpful for a time like this. I'm curious how it'll give you what you need." She was the only one who had brought her own bouquet of flowers to lay on my dad's grave. Baby's breath—her favorite.

* * *

Sometimes people became ill after letting go, as if they finally had the strength to be sick. In my case, I didn't become physically ill but became another person with unfamiliar desires. I developed an obsession with sex, like those insects that need to mate before they die. For two months, I took the train alone out to San Jose and sought out random men at nightclubs while drunk or stoned. I didn't want to go anywhere near campus, meet anyone I might run into on the way to class. The secret to success was having no standards. No requirements, no questions. The further away they were from my life, the better. It started when

I made out with a stranger against a wall at a club. A few nights later, I was grinding on a man on the dance floor, kissing him, and I gasped in shock when he reached under my dress and shoved two fingers inside me. Finally, another night, I let someone grab me by the hand and lead me to his truck, where he smoked me out. The weed, alcohol, and sex crowded my mind. Over the next few weeks, through layers of haze and disorientation, I was impressed by sex with real men. Their immanence. The crushing weight, the heat, odors, the little sounds, the moments of comedic panic or awkwardness. Bodily sensations from someone else's flesh, entire other beings, supplanted me.

One of them was younger and chattier, an Asian guy with a shaved head. Because I wasn't drunk enough, I could converse. As we sprawled across his bed after sex, he asked what I did. For once, I answered truthfully—I was a Stanford student majoring in religious studies.

When he laughed, I saw his snaggletooth, and his face was transformed. He became cute. "How did we meet?" he asked.

It immediately reminded me of when I had asked the same question of Esther: *How did we meet or live three blocks apart? Or how were we able to understand each other when we talked?* The reminder of her friendship, the fact that she lived an hour away, and the mystery of God's will called out to me across an expanse. I didn't know if she'd high-five my conquests or ask if I was okay. He wanted my number, and I shook my head.

A UTI stopped my sexual activity. All previous exhaustions were unreal compared to this one. My UAD called me in about academic probation. I saw myself as I truly was, a sore spot on the prestige of my university and the testimony of believers. Despite the miracle of getting into Stanford from my income bracket and the glut of support and opportunities, I was living proof that

God's goodness and power had limits. I had wasted so much of everyone's time and energy, that of my parents and Esther especially. All the times she came over to my house in Torrance to cheer me up, all the San Francisco adventures she planned for us, when the truth was I had no ambition to be or do anything. When I saw my mother for the funeral, she looked like she was starving. Eighty-five pounds and on the brink of osteoporosis, yet she seemed to be made of metal wires, the way she refused to give in. She seemed more likely to survive this than I did.

All I wanted to do was climb up a mountain without eating or drinking anything, until the mountain drained my life energy, and I wasted away in a crevice. No one needed to know I died. They could hope for my return until their waiting tapered off. My mind was trying to kill me, suggesting suicide at every chance. I cried on public transportation. The speed at which the outside world passed by evoked nameless associations, each too brief to hold on to. Suspended in an in-between state, sitting still yet being carried along, I became afraid I'd actually do it. *how are ya girl? everything okay?* Esther texted. I hadn't been returning her calls.

Sorry, I've been busy. Catching up with schoolwork. I didn't want to worry her. I was thankful for our physical distance, our respective classes.

wanna come hang? or i'm down to hop on caltrain.

Actually, I can't really hang for a while, sorry. I'm so behind.

Was it rock bottom because Esther couldn't be there for me? Or was rock bottom that place no one could reach?

* * *

A few weeks into Christian therapy, I resolved to quit drinking. But as I stumbled home one night, I collapsed onto a park bench for a moment because of the spins, lying down with my face smushed into the slats. I remembered pushing my face into the folds of my living room couch, begging God to comfort me. I was twelve. I had consoled my father after he cried on my shoulder, mourning the father he couldn't be for me. I'd told him it was all right, that I got my sensitivity and slowness to speak from him, that I'd get into a good college, make a lot of money, buy us a house, and make him proud. After I closed his bedroom door behind me, I crammed myself into the living room couch and called upon God. I didn't need healing, riches, or anything else. I yearned, to the point of aching, for an embrace.

I asked God, in His infinite power, to hold me, to help me feel His hug.

I waited and felt nothing.

Now at Stanford, with the cold, iron bench pressed up against my cheek, I cried out in my mind, *Where were you then?*

A breeze blew against me. With it, something else washed over me. The feeling of a groan or a scream, distinctly other. It was not my own sadness but someone else's, and startlingly vast. I heard the grief of God. God wept over me. A glimpse of cosmic, omniscient sadness.

I wept out of pity for God. I repented for assuming He wasn't there.

Slowly, I got up. I grimaced at seeing that I had stepped in dog shit, and I tried to scrape it off in the grass. A part of my dress was also tucked into my panties, from when I'd peed behind the bushes. I yanked it out.

I walked around the next few days shaken.

For the first time since my dad died, I pitied my mom. Maybe I assumed too quickly why she hit him. I thought she was punishing him for vomiting, but she might have been trying to stop him from harming himself. She should never have hit him, but what if she was desperate or scared? It was likely they didn't part on good terms—with no chance for reconciliation. When someone died, long-forgotten details surfaced, including every regret and compromised moment. How many regrets did my mother have? And the social workers hadn't found any evidence of abuse or murder; surely, they'd know how to find it.

How did God see my family—my mother and me down below, with my dead father by His side?

The other vision I had sober, on my balcony one late afternoon. I was peering over onto walkways below when I noticed a sparrow hobbling unevenly in circles. It fluttered its wings without lifting off. It persisted tirelessly, and I couldn't take my eyes off it. I worried it would be eaten by hawks, and I rushed to put on my shoes. I looked once more over the balcony to confirm its location, but it had disappeared. Had it been eaten? Had I imagined the whole thing? And still I begged God to see the sparrow, to hold it as worthy as anything.

That was when I perceived the perfect love of God. It was weighty and hovering in the northeast quadrant of the sky. It also had a directionality—toward me. Terrified, I closed my eyes and imagined myself prostrate. Surely, I'd die. I was so soiled, so cracked. Pure, perfect love would obliterate me, I'd shatter. But the love of God continued to rush toward me with a singular direction. I felt sick, with no choice but surrender.

The instant I submitted to its will, the eternal love of God entered me and filled my entire being. My body became a precious container wherein the love of God intended to stay forever. The miracle was that despite the power and holiness of divine love dwelling in me, I was not destroyed. Angels sang, hosts of celestial beings rejoiced, marveling at God's love choosing to abide in a speck of dust.

I heard my roommate's key turn the lock to our front door. She was home from lab. I nodded a hello, hurried into my bedroom, and closed the door. I stood, unable to sit or move, wondering if I was losing my mind. Was my desperate, feral, unsound mind remixing my experiences with drugs, sex, religion, and mythology in an attempt to save itself? How much consent was involved in what had just happened—did God just ravish me? I imagined how I'd sound to my professors, my classmates. But I couldn't deny the glow I felt from within, the quiet awe that became the solid ground beneath my feet. I left my dorm, treading where the sparrow had been. All the trees were reconstituted with light.

My Christian therapist blurted out that it was God ("Who else could it be?"), and then we continued our usual regimen of cognitive behavioral therapy and EMDR (which felt like small, induced visions). The members of the Bible study group I had rejoined also nodded and smiled with their hands on their chests: "God is good!" I was no longer allowed to kill myself because my body belonged to God. Of all the outlandish religious things I shared with Esther—the demon exorcisms, the speaking in tongues—my visions weren't included. I couldn't explain why not. I knew she wouldn't judge. Perhaps I feared that my faith felt qualitatively different. It was intense enough to derail our friendship. I was born again, again.

I stopped drinking and smoking. I graduated on time. "I miss drunk Miriam," Esther said on one of our walks.

When she heard me talking knowledgeably about sex at a dinner party hosted by her friends, I had to confess about my slutty era. The only other secret I kept from Esther—and also my therapist and my Bible study group—was my decision to stop masturbating, which was harder than quitting smoking. It was an intimate pact between God and me. If I ever experienced sexual pleasure again, it would be from a body, mind, and soul connection with another real human instead of the two-dimensional figures in my imagination. Soon enough, self-gratification from touch was replaced by getting off on resisting my own touch, imagining God pinning me down for His sake.

After graduating, I spent a year at home with my mom, tutored wealthy children, and applied for a master's in education. My mother's bones were responding well to her medication and physical therapy, and I wanted to fatten her up. My dream was to live quietly, teach Scripture, and have summer vacations off. When I got into San Francisco State, I asked Esther if she would room with me.

Talking to Esther in my head while delivering mail reminded me of prayer. As if Esther were no longer limited by time and space but able to hear my thoughts directly. Or like I was rambling to myself with nothing to interrupt my delusions.

Esther,

I wondered why I didn't want to kill myself after you died, when I couldn't stop thinking about it after my father's death. Would I be recognizable to you now, without my faith, without you? I don't like who I am without you. I'm unrecognizable to myself. I also can't tell who's losing their mind more—me or the world.

There was a time when I needed a solid ground beneath my feet. Then the ground gave way. I found myself balancing on a tiny surface, waves roiling under me. Is this existential core strength? Being stable seems vulgar, but suicide is off the table. Seeing what your death did to my world makes it impossible.

Esther. Did you jump off the ledge on purpose? Was there something I missed, something you hid from me? Why'd you start drinking and smoking again? Was it for fun or was there something deeper, more painful? Was it just some stupid accident? I was a bad friend. I'm sorry.

12

I tensed up when the clerk rolled the cages with the letter trays into the parking lot. They looked unusually heavy. I saw a door-to-door ad trying to lure people into switching internet providers. Great, I had to stop by every mailbox today.

A co-worker squatted down next to me. "You need help?" He used his elbow to hold one stack of letter trays while he lifted another so I could retrieve mine from the bottom. He dropped the stack with a thud.

"You can lift five trays at once?" I asked. It had taken me a month to lift three. I tried not to stare at his glove tan line—dark brown arms, pale white hands. I wondered what his wife and kids thought of his Mickey Mouse hands. I knew about his family because I'd overheard him talking to Resy. He drove two hours from Stockton every morning to deliver mail in San Francisco.

"Nah, I got back from vacation today!" he hooted. "It's crazy what a week of recovery can do. I was supposed to have two weeks off and go to Samoa with my family, but we can't go nowhere now. I might as well come back early and help with the rush."

Then Jyothi called a stand-around meeting in which everyone circled up outside, squinting in the sun as she yelled announcements. The CDC had reversed its earlier stance and was recommending masks. All carriers were to wear masks, maintain a six-foot distance from one another, and wash our hands frequently. Start times would be staggered. Everyone was given a small bottle of Purell and three white cotton masks.

"These look like little boys' underwear," someone muttered.

More than COVID, I worried about my fellow employees' knee braces, blood clots under their nails, limps, and how all of them needed or had a good masseur or acupuncturist. Resy didn't wear gloves, which meant her hands were regularly exposed to the rough edges of rusty mail openings and paper cuts. Her hands were like leather. When my own finger got caught in a metal apartment mailbox as it slammed shut, I saw one way such a purple blood clot could form. I couldn't tell if I was glad or disturbed to see my body so bruised.

Towering pallets of packages, bound in plastic, rolled in on wheels one after another. The number of online orders a quarantined city could make was tall, weighty, and pressing.

"Thirty-fifth and Thirty-sixth on eighteen are mine!" one co-worker screamed inside the station. Her forehead was wet with sweat. We turned to look as she waved a paper in another carrier's face.

"Don't talk to me like that. Boss told me it's mine." He knocked the paper out of her hand.

"Everyone knows that's my overtime! You don't get respect if you don't give it."

Resy stepped in and spoke to both of them in a low voice, at which point the other carriers resumed their work. She picked up the paper, took it to a case, and wrote something down.

"Bunch of dummies about overtime of all things," Manwai muttered as he pushed his hamper.

"Shut up, Manwai," another carrier said. "Why don't you help us instead of letting everyone else get swamped? Even the new PTF does twice the work you do."

"I put in my time already," Manwai said. "I swear this place is like a cult."

I was the new PTF, and the newer carriers were asked to do overtime first (we couldn't say no), and we got last pick of all the leftover routes. This meant the heaviest blocks with complicated traffic, construction, heavy mail, and/or steep hills. But I didn't want to be mentioned in a fight. I kept my eyes on flats I was casing.

I was restless to get out of the station, but it looked like I'd need to spend an extra hour in the office due to the volume.

In the parking lot, Resy said to me, "Don't worry. During Christmas, people fight and yell, too, but at the end of the day we're still family."

I appreciated her reassurance, but it also sounded like something a cult leader would say.

*   *   *

Number 827 Twenty-ninth Avenue was a two-story goldenrod house with bougainvillea winding up one side. The first floor was mainly the garage, and a long flight of stairs led up to the front door, as was the case with most homes on this hilly street. But instead of having their mail opening on the ground level in the garage door, this house required me to climb the stairs and bend down to the slot at the bottom of the front door. As I walked up the steps, I felt the burn in my quads and was tempted to throw the mail up, letters and magazines fluttering down in a cascade.

The door opened, and a middle-aged woman with curly sandy hair called out to me, "Hey! Excuse me."

"Hi, how are you?" I was filled with resentful, ignoble thoughts about her and her house until the reality of her presence flustered me. Thankfully, my mask covered my blushing face.

"I got notification that a package was delivered, but I can't find it." She showed me the email on her phone from inside her door. "It's a really important package—the masks I ordered from Etsy." She crossed her arms.

I remembered a soft package from Etsy, and my energy faltered. "I'm sorry, let me check if I accidentally delivered to 827 one street over. I'm really sorry about that." I wasn't sure, but it was a possibility. I'd have to stop delivering, walk back to the vehicle, drive over to the other street, and knock on the door. It was my fault. I hoped someone was home.

"I can't believe this! You know how long I've been waiting for that package? I can't leave the house without a mask."

"I'm sorry. I'll check right now and get back to you."

"Unbelievable." She slammed the door in my face.

Of the thousands of packages I'd delivered, I'd made one mistake (that I knew of). She spoke to me as if I were a delinquent, forgetting that I was risking my health for her safety. I bent down and slid her letters through the slot. *You're welcome, bitch!* I thought to myself. I couldn't believe the annoying personality of the mail slot matched its owner.

But she needed those masks. And I'd messed up.

As I drove to the previous street, I thought about quitting. Maybe I should go back to teaching—secular education, tutoring rich kids. I didn't need to suffer like this. If I charged $50 an hour, how many students would I need? My co-workers might shake their heads thinking, *Miriam was fast, but she burned out. What a disappointment.* I'd become just a customer again.

I groaned to see that the other 827 looked abandoned. There was an overgrown lawn and car covered in rust. As for the house, the paint was chipping away, curtains drawn, no sign of life. The Etsy package had been small enough to fit through the mail slot. I knocked on the door. As I waited, I remembered that rainy day at Esther's apartment, how I'd banged on her door, hoping she was hungover inside. Her family, the trash bags, her mother's scream.

"Hey, are you the new carrier for this route?"

I looked up, dazed. A white-haired Asian man stood on the sidewalk in front of the abandoned house.

"There, there. I know delivering mail is tough. I used to be a carrier. You must be a PTF."

I wiped my face on the pugs.

"You'll get used to it. How long you been delivering?"

"A month or two." Those girls complaining and drinking wine were right. Time had no meaning.

I glanced at my vehicle. Mail and packages baked inside. Even more time away from delivering mail. When would I get home tonight?

"If you ever need to use the bathroom or need water, feel free to stop by. My wife and I live in that purple house right there. She was a carrier, too. We got to look out for each other. The postal service is still like family to us."

I glanced up at his house. An Asian lady with a gray bob waved out the window. I waved back.

I drove back to the bougainvillea house. I told the woman no one was home, but I would check again at the end of the day, and every day until I got ahold of them.

She peered through the cracked-open door. I stood a respectful six feet away. "I already ordered more masks. Express with FedEx." She closed the door without a goodbye. I had neither the time nor the heart to tell her that we delivered residential express packages for FedEx. Thankfully, the postal service no longer required signatures. I wouldn't have to see her face again.

*   *   *

On the way back to the station, I saw yet another moving van. Three young men carried a couch toward it. It was the third moving van I'd seen that day, the fifth that week. College students whose classes were canceled or young people who couldn't afford to live in the city anymore and were being forced to move. More upheavals.

*   *   *

When I got back to the station, I was surprised to see a small pin in my case, accompanied by a note of gratitude from the San Francisco district manager. The pin, shaped like a puzzle piece, was made of shiny red enamel, its edges outlined in gold. In the middle, small golden letters spelled out YOU ARE ESSENTIAL. The fashion designer for the postal service made everything so cute. I pinned it onto my visor.

Some of my co-workers rolled their eyes, and one of them taped the note up to his case with a sarcastic note: *What a joke.*

I asked that co-worker if I could have his pin. He shrugged and handed it to me. I pinned it to my collar. Manwai wore his pinned to his surgical mask.

*   *   *

The next day at the station, I was approached by a Chinese woman with an accent. She didn't wear a uniform but wore something my mother would—black cargo pants, a collared flower-print shirt, and a visor. It looked like she had wandered into the station from an Asian supermarket. She carried a clipboard. "Are you route ten?"

I nodded.

She showed me a missing-package report. My stomach sank. It was another one, not the Etsy masks. I must have been really out of it. She showed me a map of where my barcode scanner said the package was delivered to and where the package should have gone. She asked if I remembered delivering the package, and if I could go back today and try to find it. I could ask the residents of the house I delivered it to or look around the bushes or the gates where I dropped it off.

I promised I would. "I'm so sorry."

"It's okay. Everyone makes mistakes. Just try to find it."

Then she went off looking for another carrier. That was her whole job. To chase down carriers on behalf of packages reported missing.

*   *   *

One unspoken rule of Amazon Sunday was never to leave anyone out late alone to become an easy target for our supervisor. A few write-ups and a carrier could be suspended without pay. So on Sundays, we delivered our own routes, then helped one another. At the end of the day, our mail truck caravan, like a line of baby ducklings, headed back to the station together. Ayesha and I had the smallest vehicles, so we were expected to finish first and start helping others earlier. But even with the smaller vehicle and fewer packages, Ayesha always needed the most help, even more than the carriers who drove the larger Pro Vans. One Sunday, I drove up to her LLV and parked on the corner of Point Lobos and Forty-fifth where the road dropped out of sight over a hill toward the ocean. I remembered that Ayesha lived in Oakland and wasn't as familiar as I was with San Francisco, where I'd lived for ten years. She was also the only Black mail carrier among all Asians on Sundays, and I didn't want her to feel left out. But when I got to her vehicle, I couldn't find her. No one was in the driver's seat. The surrounding streets were empty. Her vehicle was deserted.

I was about to leave and help another co-worker when the partition inside her vehicle cleared to the side. Ayesha stooped to the front and slid the front door open.

"I didn't know you'd get here so fast." She held two small plastic baggies filled with a creamy liquid. She dumped them into her small cooler, with other similarly filled baggies.

"What's that?"

"Milk."

"To deliver?"

She laughed. "No, I have to pump every few hours."

I felt stupid.

She continued, "With setup and cleanup, it takes half an hour each time, too. I can't do anything while I'm pumping but sit there."

I considered this in light of the recent onslaught of packages. Ayesha should have been exempt from overtime, not one of the first to do the worst of it. I didn't say this out loud. Instead, I asked, "How old is your baby?"

"Four months old. You have kids?"

"No. But I want to." I didn't know if it was still true.

"How old are you?"

"Thirty-three."

"I was gonna say no need to rush because they completely change your life, but . . . You can when you can."

She picked up a black bag and was about to close it when I asked, "Can I see?"

"My breast pump?"

I nodded. I had never seen one before.

With one hand she gripped thin tubes and a bottle with a suction cup attached to it. She looked curious about my curiosity.

"It's so mechanical," I said. The plastic containers had dregs of milk left in them. I thought for a moment how these bodily fluids were recently a part of her. I turned away. It felt too personal.

We discussed which streets of hers I should take. I grabbed a third of her packages, a shelf and three bins' worth. An hour later, I texted the group, *Who's next?*

Then I received a call from an unknown number.

"Hello, this is San Francisco Animal Control, may I please speak to Miriam Lee?"

"This is she."

"Do you own a dog at 2226 Thirty-seventh Avenue? There have been complaints about loud barking for hours throughout the day."

My stomach soured. "Yeah, he's in my backyard while I work."

"Does your dog have a shelter when it rains and access to drinking water? And do you feed him regularly?"

"Yes."

"So technically, we're not allowed to do anything as long as the dog has access to water and shelter outside. Dogs are allowed to bark. We're just making sure he's not in distress. After ten P.M., it becomes a disturbance issue, but that's SFPD's jurisdiction."

After we hung up, I thought about my neighbors trapped in their homes with Dolmangi's incessant barking. I almost teared up thinking of Dolmangi's anxiety and loneliness. He had no idea there was a pandemic and an inordinate number of packages.

When I got back to the station around six in the evening, one of the carriers walked up to me. "You should hurry up and learn to drive the Pro Van. I'll tell Jyothi to schedule you for a training."

The Pro Vans intimidated me because they were so sleek and shiny, and I was endeared to the loud, shaky metal boxes of the LLVs. But I knew I had to learn how to drive the Pro Van. The volume of packages was only getting worse. People were not only ordering groceries, diapers, toilet paper, and water, but seemed to be redecorating every room in their homes. Lamps, shelves, rugs, exercise equipment, weights—I wanted to scream, "Just order what you *need*!"

I had decided to call up Patty, to ask if she and Minyoung might watch Dolmangi while I delivered mail. Dolmangi liked them, and their nickname for him was "our little gentleman." I had avoided them for long enough, and I wondered what their relationship was like now that they'd moved in with each other.

I was still wearing my uniform in my breakfast nook when I heard Patty's voice over the phone. I'd last heard it over a month ago, in a Zoom recording of our grief group.

"Miriam!" The excitement in her voice moved me because of its legitimate claim: we were friends. It felt like I was hearing her voice from a distant country, one where we saw each other regularly. She lived a fifteen-minute walk away, where Esther used to live.

"Patty! How are you holding up?"

"We're doing fine, I guess." The committed-relationship first-person plural. "How are you? How's delivering mail?"

"Super-busy. We're slammed."

"Oh, right! I think of you every time I see our mailman."

I smiled. "How is it living with Minyoung?"

"It doesn't really feel like I have a roommate half the day. I wake up super-early, and she goes to bed super-late, and we sleep in separate rooms."

My stomach turned. "Minyoung's sleeping in Esther's old room?"

"Yeah. She did a whole ceremony, lighting incense and candles, playing her favorite music, pouring drinks. Minyoung moved the bed to a different wall. She made a pretty altar for Esther, too. Designed it and got it custom-made from an artisan woodworker. I'll send you a picture."

I breathed a long breath out. I could see Minyoung sleeping in Esther's old room, not avoiding the empty spaces, but acknowledging them and keeping them company. She was the type of person who could befriend her own sadness and materialize it into ritual and art. We all interacted with Esther's absence in our own ways.

"How are you and Dolmangi doing?" Patty asked.

"Actually, I have a favor to ask." I explained the situation, and she was happy to do it. They had recently painted some walls and furniture, and asked if Dolmangi could come in a couple of days when everything had dried. We talked about a desire to see each other outdoors, and I meant it, though I was honest about my work schedule.

After we hung up, Patty sent me the picture of Esther's altar. On the wall hung a smooth, upright dark panel of wood with its edges curled like smoke along its whorled grain. A shelf jutted out and held a framed picture: Esther backlit and in profile, sitting on a bench at a campsite, knees folded and tucked into a large sweater. She dragged on a cigarette, and the low rays of a morning sun gleamed through wisps of smoke and fog. I had taken the picture. Next to the picture was a tiny vase with baby's breath, Esther's air-dry clay incense burner, and a Dodgers shot glass filled with dark liquid.

Patty texted a note, *Minyoung gives Esther a little coffee every morning. And when we're drinking beer, she pours some for Esther, too.*

I remembered the signs Minyoung picked up after Esther died. The butterfly that landed and lingered on Minyoung's shoulder during the group picture after the funeral, or how right when we were reminiscing about Esther's love for her dog, Maggie, Esther's framed painting of Maggie fell to the floor. Minyoung believed in the afterlife, in spirits. On the other side now, I felt envy and pained nostalgia. I had no idea what was real anymore, no assurance or certainty about where or what Esther was. But I liked it for Minyoung, and I appreciated her closeness to Esther. I understood too well the impulse for acts of devotion.

I texted Patty and Minyoung back, *The altar is beautiful. Please let Esther and Dolmangi say hi to each other there.*

13

When Esther and I were roommates in the Excelsior neighborhood, I had classes in the mornings and tutoring in the afternoons, and she was a barista at a café that turned into a bar at night. By my second year of grad school, her late-night binges increasingly messed with my sleep.

One night, she'd thrown her hands up in frustration. "Spit it out. What are you mad about?"

I couldn't answer. I felt physically unable to speak.

"Then stop stinking up the whole room with your attitude. Every time I come into the kitchen you can't even look at me. You look constipated. Then you leave two minutes later without saying anything. When I ask what's wrong, you say nothing, and it makes me feel fucking crazy."

I told Esther it was probably because I had been trained not to speak as a child. Whereas Esther had been surrounded by so much noise that she had learned to shout to be heard.

"Okay, but you're still passive-aggressive as fuck," she went on. "Something is leaking, and it stinks. I can't read your mind."

"I wish you wouldn't stomp around late at night," I forced myself to say. "You can tiptoe while I'm sleeping. I would for you."

Esther listened, her face still. "Anything else?"

"Try to notice how much of my food you're eating versus how much of yours I eat." A week until my next paycheck, I had been monitoring my account after each purchase, making sure I didn't overdraft. "I don't want to do tit for tat, but just *notice*. Like, I appreciate how you wash the dishes when I cook, but I buy way more groceries, and you eat more of my leftovers. Don't just think about what you can take, think about what you give, too. Don't be a *yamchae*."

"What's that?"

"Someone who shows up to a potluck with only chopsticks." When I was growing up, my family had been dependent on the charity of others, on taxpayers and government programs. I was afraid of being a *yamchae* my whole life. I admired the uncalculating, carefree way Esther shared and received, but I was irritated by her lack of guilt or mindfulness.

"But I always ask before I eat your food. Every time you said, 'Go for it.' Or 'Eat whatever you want.'"

"I guess I didn't mean it," I was embarrassed to say.

"Okay." She shifted her weight from one leg to the other. "Do you know you don't mean it when you say it? Or are you figuring that out now?"

"Now." I imagined how annoying this must be. "I'm sorry."

"How about all the other nice things you say or do for me? How can I tell if you mean it or if you'll be pissed at me later?"

I took a deep breath. "I'll have to think harder before I offer anything now." I winced at how bad that sounded.

She shook her head and mumbled, "You're not such a saint after all."

"No." In my head, I heard my mother's voice, *What did you do to deserve to cry?*

"Why do I feel like you're always judging me these days?"

"I never said that."

"Why do you look at me like I'm garbage?"

"I do?"

Her voice shook. "Miriam. I know your face."

"I don't think you're garbage! You're a hard worker . . . and you can spend your free time however you want." I could hear the rancor in my words. And I knew Esther wouldn't be wrong about my facial expression.

She knew it, too. "I need to go."

I sat there in the breakfast nook remembering how willingly she'd come over without judgment or commentary when I needed her. Out of everyone in the world, I was the last one allowed to think of her as a nuisance. Besides, I had been the one with my head in the toilet in the evening, hungover with her in the morning, splitting a pint of ice cream for brunch until my dad died and God saved my life. I had been scared to ask myself what I really thought of her dropping stuff, bumping into furniture, vomiting loudly into the toilet at three in the morning, her playing music in the middle of the night (even with her head-phones on, I could hear it), her daylong hangovers in bed. How she'd get up only to go out again, her hour-long baths when I needed to take a shit, all her hairs clogging the shower drain, all the times I vacuumed and mopped and she didn't. Cooking and cleaning without help or thanks made me her servant, which reminded me of my childhood. But Esther never asked for it. She could comfortably live in squalor, whereas clutter and grime too easily made my mind and mood feel out of order.

My childhood apartment had so many building violations it no longer qualified to be government housing, but all the other low-income apartments in our area had wait lists in the hundreds. My mom faced homelessness until a social worker miraculously, and maybe illegally, helped her skip the lines. The need to take care of my mother in the future weighed on me. Whereas Esther seemed to have no plan for her future. I knew her brothers were on her about her lack of a long-term job.

It was four A.M. when she got home that night. I heard her collapse into bed. No bathroom, no water, just bed.

The next morning around nine, as I was leaving to catch the bus, she walked into the kitchen from the fire escape, holding a mug and a weed roach. She closed the door behind her and collapsed onto the floor. The handle of the mug broke into a splatter of lukewarm tea, and she convulsed with her eyes rolled back.

I moved toward her instinctively, setting aside the broken mug with a kitchen towel, checking her breath and pulse. I smoothed her bangs and put my hand on her forehead—cold and clammy. After spasming on the floor, Esther settled into a peaceful repose, except her arms and legs were splayed in disturbing angles. I squatted beside her and felt a rush of anxiety and anger.

"Esther."

She slowly opened her eyes. Her gaze was unfocused. Then she closed them again.

I checked my watch.

"Esther, let's lie down in bed."

I reached under her armpits and sat her up. She acquiesced when lifted and leaned on me as we wobbled to her bedroom and landed on her bed. Her motor control seemed to have returned, judging by the way she rolled onto her side and tucked her legs into a fetal position. I wondered if the weed did this or something else. After watching her fall asleep, I wrote Esther a sticky note about her seizure (in case she didn't remember) and my concern for her health.

*   *   *

On the bus, I thought how Esther had looked while spasming on the floor. I didn't need to see that at nine in the morning, and what was in her spliff? What if she was having a stroke? Should I have taken her to the hospital, or would that have been overkill? On my phone, I searched *Can weed give you a seizure?* Whom was she going out with these days? There were her co-workers at the café, her old friends from school, anyone I didn't know?

Then I thought about the party we had gone to in the Marina the week before. A church member was throwing a rooftop party there, and I'd invited Esther, partly to repay her for all the SF State parties she had invited me to, partly to introduce her to my people. Bringing Esther made me notice acutely that my church had a lot of tech bros, former high school quarterbacks, and people wearing Patagonia. But there was also rosé, a nice charcuterie board, and a string of lights overhead. Above all, these were people who believed in my visions. Because I was a deaconess, a Sunday school volunteer, and a leader of a women's Bible study, everyone at the party knew me, and I could tell who was new. So many of them had heard about Esther and were excited to meet her.

While I was stuck in a conversation about repurposing floppy disks as coasters, Esther unplugged a laptop from the speakers and plugged in her iPod. She blasted Velvet Underground at the highest volume, and everyone stared at her as she smoked a cigarette while leaning over the balcony. Even the pedestrians walking below glanced up at Esther, who looked right back at them. Whenever someone tried to lower the volume or unplug her iPod, Esther groaned loudly, stomped back to the speakers, replugged her iPod, and cranked up the volume. I knew that no one from my church would try to change the music after that, and despite myself, I struggled to hold in a laugh.

It was the part of Esther that was the most different from me, the part of her I was drawn to. Since high school, she had volunteered with kids with disabilities. She connected with their honesty and found endearing how openly they expressed affection or frustration. Sometimes she was embarrassed by her own lack of social ease and confused by certain looks and silences that made her feel like she had something on her face. The potential dismay of my church friends receded into the background. Esther was right. It was a boring party, the exact type of party she hated. But when I asked if she wanted to leave, she replied, "I want to finish listening to my mix."

I got off the bus to transfer to another line and wondered how Esther and I had become friends in the first place. Whether in front of her boss or a five-year-old, she was the same person. She was generously and vulnerably herself at all times, without guile or artifice, whereas blending in was my primary defense. I tried to become whatever each situation or crowd demanded, giving in to other people's expectations and desires at my expense, to the point that I didn't know who I was or if I had a self at all. How much could I ask Esther to bend to my comfort? Or should I be the one to loosen up? Patty told me we simply weren't meant to live together, that our friendship would return to normal if we lived separately.

When I got home, her handwriting was scrawled on the edge of my sticky note: *work today / talk when I get back / I got dinner*

* * *

Esther spread out containers of kale salad and mushroom pizza from her café on the table. I felt a mix of gratitude for her response to my criticism and embarrassment that I'd shamed her into bringing me food. "First of all, sorry for what happened this morning," she said. "I don't know what it was. I feel fine now though. Did I look bad?"

"Yeah, it definitely wasn't normal. Do you remember it?"

"Sort of." She drizzled hot sauce over her slice. "Something fucked-up happened last night."

I wasn't sure if she meant our argument. "What do you mean?"

"I think I sexually assaulted someone."

"What?" After the initial shock, I assumed she was being paranoid. Even at her drunkest, she would never hurt anyone. Likely the other guy wanted it—Esther was hot. "Are you sure?"

"I don't remember the whole night, but . . . I know I was drinking with some co-workers. I have this memory of riding in some souped-up lowriders with some old Mexican dudes in the Mission. You know, those dudes in the cowboy hats and the vintage cars? It was a convertible . . . I think." She held back her bangs from her forehead. "I must've asked them to take me for a spin. Maybe that's when I split from Anton and Tricia."

"Sounds fun." I was relieved we were talking again.

"No." She was serious. "I shouldn't get into strangers' cars drunk and alone. It scares me that I did. I'm lucky they were nice."

"It's all right. Nothing bad happened. And your friends shouldn't have let you go off by yourself either." I worried that our fight had caused her to drink as much as she did.

Then she groaned and put her forehead on the table, her ponytail landing in the kale salad. "Fuck!"

"What's wrong? What happened?"

"I saw my dispensary crush on the bus."

"The bald one?" He was the shy and quiet one with sleepy, bedtime eyes. He stooped unassumingly inside the dispensary that shone black lights and blasted techno music.

"Yeah."

"Is he the one you think you sexually assaulted?"

"I can't go to that dispensary ever again. I fucking hate myself."

"What happened?"

"Wait, I don't want to think about it right now. Can we finish our food first?"

As we ate together in silence, I understood Esther still didn't feel comfortable around me. Her venting had more to do with her stress. I could have been anyone.

"Don't. I'll clean up." As if she were demonstrating her fulfillment of my demands.

I sat still.

"Okay," she continued. "On the bus, I saw my crush. I sat next to him. I think he recognized me, and I think we kissed. Then I think I tried to unzip his pants or get my hands down them or something in front of everyone." She groaned. "Then he got up, and I followed him off the bus. On the sidewalk, I tried to kiss him, but he pulled back and gave me a sad smile. I think he said, 'You're a sweet girl,' but he has an accent, and I was drunk, so maybe it was something else. Then he left."

I was quiet. "I don't know if that counts as assault."

"But if a guy did that to me—"

"Well, you said y'all were kissing first?"

"I'm not sure." She looked sick.

"'Sweet girl' isn't something you say to an assailant."

"Maybe he was trying to reject me nicely so I wouldn't do something crazier. Remember that strung-out Asian lady we saw on the bus the other day, feeling up that old white dude?"

"Yeah." She wore dirty clothes, had greasy hair, and kept asking him for five dollars.

"I'm like her."

"No, you're not. Or we all are." We were all made in God's image.

"Shut up, Miriam." Esther pressed her palms against her eyes. "I feel so bad, so sorry to him."

"First of all, how many people are on the bus that late at night? They were probably sleeping or drunk anyways. Remember how that white guy shouted, 'Bitch stole my weed!' after that Asian lady stumbled away from him? No one on the bus turned their head. Nobody gives a shit. It's the city—all sorts of things happen. And maybe you're not remembering it correctly. Maybe he was into it and felt you up, too. You have to admit you don't know what happened."

"He didn't feel me up. I sexually assaulted an Arab immigrant in public. He probably thinks this country is full of nut bags."

She aggressively cleared the table, shoving everything back into the plastic bag.

"I think you're okay."

No response.

"Thanks for dinner."

"Uh-huh."

*   *   *

I never saw Esther collapse again, but she no longer touched my food. I wondered if she got over what happened that night because she didn't slow down. She no longer stomped when she came home, but her footsteps still reverberated in our old unit. I bought earplugs. It was an uneasy truce.

Then there was a rat infestation.

The rats ripped open our cereal boxes and established their dominance over the kitchen with a fetid smell. Esther avoided the situation completely. She wasn't home much anyway, but she accepted that we no longer had a kitchen and kept her door closed. I was the one calling the landlord, buying traps, vacuuming the rat shit, and mopping the floors of that rat piss smell. Esther only came home to sleep, and sometimes she texted me that she was crashing with friends. In the middle of the day, when a rat the size of my forearm ran across the kitchen floor and squeezed under the oven, my resentment toward Esther flared up. Everything about the way the rat wriggled felt wrong. The landlord finally sent exterminators, but the rats kept returning. When I caught Esther coming in and out of the apartment, I worried because she didn't look healthy, which irritated me even more. Why wasn't she taking care of herself? She had bags under her eyes and her skin was breaking out. Like my mother, she had lost a lot of weight. I wanted to offer her my kimchi stew or fried rice but felt too cowardly and bitter to do so.

A month later, I wasn't surprised when she told me she wasn't interested in renewing the lease. She was going to volunteer at a hostel in Nashville in exchange for room and board. Around when she sold her bed and her desk, I started to panic about our friendship. After all we had been through, we would be broken up by domestic labor disputes. I wrote her a letter, saying that I wasn't ready for our friendship to end. Even if she moved, I wanted to figure out how to make it work because we were family. If she ran away, I wouldn't let her out of my life. I'd find her.

She sat across from me in the kitchen nook. "I read your letter," she said, her voice tired. "But I need some space first. Hope that's okay." If this was Esther's rock bottom, she wasn't letting me in, and I didn't know what to do. I had become the straightedge, and Esther was a wreck. What was the point of feeling on top of things if Esther wasn't there, happy, with me?

14

Resy had warned me about postal service spies: supervisors and postmasters who drove around in street clothes and regular cars to snoop on lowly mail carriers. They mostly went out on Sundays, since fewer carriers were delivering, and the newer carriers made the most mistakes and had the fewest protections. If you got caught breaking the same rule twice, it was suspension without pay, or for someone on probation such as me—termination.

A silver Ford Taurus trailed behind me slowly, and when I parked, it stopped with the engine on. When I returned to the vehicle after delivering four packages, the Ford's engine was off, and a gray-haired, tall white man and another older Latina stepped out. He wore a white woven polo shirt, she a long-sleeve button-down. Both wore lanyards around their necks with postal service IDs.

"I'm Don with the postal service, and this is Eva. Do you have your ID on you?"

I took it out of my back pocket. He inspected it and handed it back to me. Then he walked over to my vehicle, opened the side door, and peered inside. The woman watched. I felt like I was in trouble, but I couldn't think of anything I did wrong.

In the gentlest voice the man said, "Your emergency lights aren't on. When you're double-parked, they should be."

Older carriers warned me that the ancient LLV batteries could die if I kept the emergency lights on, but I said, "Okay."

"You see this?" He picked up a dusty triangular wooden block from behind my driver's seat. It appeared to have been painted red a thousand years ago. "You know what this is?"

He had to be kidding. No one used those blocks. "Yes, it's for the tires."

Pointing down the length of the street, he said, "You see, we're on an incline. These brakes have given out before. Show me where you're supposed to put it."

As he handed it to me, I didn't know if I wanted to hide the exasperation on my face or if he deserved to see that he was harassing his workers while failing to appreciate or protect us. I placed the triangular block behind the closest rear wheel.

"There, now it won't roll back down the hill. What if a child was playing there?"

What if we had functioning vehicles with safe brakes? What if they finally replaced vehicles that were older than time? And practically every street in San Francisco had a slope.

"She doesn't have any dog spray," the lady pointed out.

"I never received dog spray."

"What station do you—"

"That's all right," the man interrupted. "That's not your fault. Make sure to get one from your supervisor immediately. Where's your satchel?"

"It's Amazon Sunday. We don't have any mail."

"You should be wearing your satchel at all times."

"Even when it's empty?"

"That's correct."

If I weren't a mail carrier, I would find the humor and even charm in the absurdity. But I had hundreds of packages to deliver, and I didn't want to wear an empty satchel for no reason, nor put a wooden block behind my tire every time I left the vehicle. The expectation of silent compliance reminded me of living under my mother's roof, and I thought I had already served my eighteen-year sentence. I heard Ayesha's voice in my head: *I . . . hate . . . my . . . job!* Everyone broke every rule in the handbook at every moment to deliver mail on time. If I followed the handbook, I'd be out delivering packages until midnight, and then they'd chew me up for costing them in overtime pay.

"Let's see you deliver now, correctly." They sat in their Ford and watched me like they were at a drive-in movie theater.

I staged the next three packages for delivery. I clicked in my seat belt and closed the side door—something I never did unless I was leaving from the station or driving back to it. I rolled a few yards, the silver Ford following behind me. Then I turned off my engine, turned on my emergency lights, undid my seat belt, picked up the wooden block, put it behind the rear wheel. I went back to the front, put on an empty satchel, and gathered the three packages. After I delivered them, they watched me take the block back in, drive a little farther, and do it all again. Finally they slipped away, the lady giving me a thumbs-up from her passenger window as she passed by. I would have given her a different finger myself. I immediately texted the Amazon Sunday group chat.

postal inspectors out today. silver Ford Taurus. I told them everything they inspected me for.

fuccckkkkkk

those bastards

Throughout the day, each of my co-workers shared about their raids and sent memes of people screaming, even the immigrant dad in his forties, which made me laugh. Everyone else's inspections went more smoothly because they put on their satchels, dog spray, emergency lights, and parking brakes (which the Pro Vans had). As soon as any of us were inspected, we went back to delivering as usual, but the stops slowed us down considerably. By the time we returned to the station, the moon was high in the sky. Dolmangi was likely hoarse from barking.

As we returned to the station, one behind the other, parked our vehicles, and emerged with our arms full of empty bins, I felt a pang of closeness and camaraderie. They knew nothing about Esther or my family, and I knew nothing of their personal dramas. But we knew what we went through today. We shared the same type of physical labor and frustrations, and for the first time in a long time, I felt comforted.

* * *

Delivering on Amazon Sundays familiarized each mail carrier with the defining quirks of each route in their station. If carriers graduated from Amazon Sundays or were old enough to remember delivering mail before Amazon, their knowledge of all the other routes in our zip code came from years of covering routes for carriers on vacation, sick, or injured. We all knew which routes were shitty or easy-breezy. The notorious ones were long, had steep hills, many packages, and busy streets that were hard to cross. One particularly evil route had stairs to every front door, with low mail slots near the ground, which was like doing a StairMaster and squats with weights, hundreds of times a day. The easy routes were short, had barely any packages, and had perfectly placed mail openings. The oldest carriers, with the most seniority, nabbed them, which earned them the nickname *retirement routes*. This seemed fair.

This level of knowledge extended to the intimacy with which all regular carriers memorized every name and address they delivered to. They knew which families on their streets were expecting babies, which couples went through divorce, which were running small businesses from their homes.

But we and our work were largely unknown to our customers as we slipped by and dropped things off. We rustled in and out, through front lawns, back gates, up their stairs, onto porches, inserting things daily into familiar orifices, unseen. Occasionally a customer chased me down to hand me some outgoing mail or got to know my name, but most of the attention was one-way.

With all our revenue coming from postage and business ads, no tax dollars went to paying postal service employees or refurbishing equipment, which was why our hampers, shelves, and vehicles were decrepit. The postal service was asked to stand on its own while being accessible to all. This was part of its charm and sadness—a service not driven by profits or recognition; the dire need of updates, resources, support, and streamlining; the financial and operational mismanagement by distant authorities. The only witness to the postal service was itself.

* * *

On a Tuesday, I thought I saw Esther from behind. She never owned a chunky mustard-colored knit sweater, but she could have. It was paired with boot-cut jeans and a loping gait, shoulder-length brown hair bouncing in the sun—I couldn't take my eyes off her.

I realized I wouldn't feel betrayed if Esther had faked her death and disappeared. Despite the wreckage of her departure, I realized I wouldn't chase her down and find her. I would be grateful to the point of bowing to the ground if only she were alive.

This woman was much younger, with a bigger face and smaller mouth. She didn't see the mail carrier crying in her direction.

miriam,

sorry for the late response; your email's been sittin pretty in my draft box cuz i wasnt sure what to write to you about.

here in nashville, i mostly sit at the front desk and clean the hostel. it was kinda like double dutch at first, i was trying to get into the rhythm of how everything worked. i became familiar with names/ personalities and got a better idea of the environment i work in; it feels kinda cliquey but there are some nice peeps/ no ones really an asshole, so im trying to navigate it as best as i can.

i dig the living situation. we have a backyard with really long weeds and grass, but we have a section of cement and patio furniture so its a dope spot to have a cigarette. we also got a little stoop in the front which is nice to have a smoke on sunny days.

ive been listening to the blues a lot these days, it makes me feel things/ the struggles of being human and spirituality, which reminded me of you . . . i attached a couple of youtube videos of the songs if you wanted to have a listen.

i feel as i get older i find it harder to form new friendships; i dont know why but i relate less to the new people i encounter and vice versa?

i needed to get out of the city and do something drastic to wake myself up. im sorry about the note we left on too. i need to work on myself and im figuring out what i want to do. i hope going back to therapy goes well for you. let me know if you learn anything useful in that boundaries book.

all in all, im trying to find a groove and feel comfortable with myself without making other people feel uncomfortable. its a struggle but i hope to find that medium.

things have been chill for the most part, these few months alone already feels pretty adult: paying healthcare bills, student loans, phone bill, filing taxes. i kinda dig the responsibilities.

there was this guy i was working with, a quiet, laid back, thoughtful guy. he reads a lot. i spend most of my breaks and evenings with him, and we finally slept together the other night. he said we should have done this a long time ago. it's sad because he leaves for new york in a week.

hope you enjoy the music.

-esther

* * *

Other than the letters we wrote to each other in high school, we had mostly texted. But that one year of long distance had produced longer streams of her living voice. The next time I heard from her, several months later, she was back in our hometown, Torrance.

miriam,

i was so scared to come back home cuz i had nothing lined up and knew that i could get stuck there in the meantime. im kinda mad at myself for letting that happen because ive been so damn unproductive and unmotivated for so long, especially cuz my skin has been freaking out and in response ive been freaking out about my skin and its kinda gotten me down. man, this adult acne is a shit stain on my self-esteem. i wanna cry n laugh at the same time cuz i feel no one wants to hire someone with acne, yet its so silly how much its made a difference in what i can/want to do. but im def at the point where i gotta move forward than being idle. got some real talk from my brothers; they told me that not everyone gets to do what they want, and i gotta buck up and think about establishing something for my future.

its weird being home and im tryin to plan my escape outta here. tho job opportunities are tumbleweeds up in this biznatch.

i had a phone interview for the golden ticket job of being a park ranger last week, but i bombed that shit. i had a hard time stringing together sentences, i just sounded like a bumbling idiot. i hate/ am horrible at open ended/ situational questions and i get so frustrated with myself because i cant help it. i psyche myself out because i dont know the zing word in the question to give a competent answer on the spot. ok i dont wanna beat myself up too hard on it cuz it already happened, but its something i know i need to work on for future job interviews.

im also thinking of finding something in the east bay cuz i heard the city is getting ridiculous with rent, and i feel a slower pace of urban life is a better fit for me at the moment. Though i only have lukewarm feelings about moving back up north. all i know is i gotta start a life of my own outside my parents home whether it be in close proximity or up north. but i think i needed this time to muddle through this shit cuz it made me face my own flaws and how it affects my relationships with people i love. so i guess theres a reason for why all this has happened. im glad to finally find some sort of conclusion for what the past year has been; im gonna be ok haha.

its also strange cuz even tho im dyin to get outta here, im also scared. maybe cuz i dont wanna live far away from my fam. i dunno, its this big guilt i have leavin the la area. i dunno, im pretty disappointed in myself n where im at, i dont wanna make excuses of woulda, coulda, shoulda. i just gotta do it . . . and thats why i think i need to get outta here cuz im just not bein a productive person. ugh readin everything i wrote, such first world problems.

ive been driving my dad's old celica, and socal freeways make me feel like a stressed cat behind the wheel. but otherwise a car has sanctuary like qualities. if theres one place i enjoy solitude, its a car.

ive actually been checking out some churches for some spiritual healing. i really liked lighthouse. you should come visit. i miss you.

-esther

I visited her in Torrance a year after she moved out of our apartment. I'd finished grad school, and she was working a temporary gig at a center for adults with disabilities, driving them around town and leading them on guided activities such as grocery shopping, pasta making, and papier-mâché. The first day we met up, the sky was neon gray regardless of the sun's position. We sat in her backyard at the mosaic table we called Café Esther. We each had a mug of concentrated coffee, cigarettes in hand.

"It's been interesting staying with my parents," she said. "I can see so much more of myself in them. I get why my dad does what he does, why he explodes and shuts down, how he feels trapped and wants to go on a binge." She hunched forward. "I understand him on another level but . . . I . . . really don't want to be like him." Her eyes rested on the oak tree in front of us. Her usual bounce and frisk were replaced with an unsentimental hardness.

"I want to change." She took in a deep breath, and her exhale was shaky. She sounded unsure, but her face looked determined. No makeup on her face, her eyelashes downcast. Her soul seemed stripped bare. Esther didn't have any visions, any conversations with God. She wrestled with herself alone. It hurt to see how long solitude had made her so tentative, yet she wanted to reengage, put herself out there.

In that moment, all I could think was how beautiful she was.

*   *   *

Esther,

You left in the middle of your searching. You were always looking for meaning. You left before getting over your insecurities and fears, but you were getting closer.

For years, every time you thought you saw the guy from the bus, you cringed or even let out a loud groan. You stayed haunted by your past. When you began substitute teaching, you would regret every time you thought one of your students saw you smoking outside school. I told you no one cared, but you were sensitive about it. Despite your punk rock attitude, at times you couldn't stand the thought of others looking down on you or thinking you were a freak.

I wish I could have seen you become an ajumma. An old lady at peace with herself. A grandma who was still searching, but with a growing treasure trove of experiences, music, and ideas she found along the way. I wish you had more time to live free from shame. Not that you didn't know freedom. I wish I could have seen you even a day older than you were. I miss you. I love you forever.

*   *   *

A stamp, then our addresses and names handwritten in serif font. My Sharpie crossed out the stamp and wrote *dec*. I put it in the front pocket of my satchel along with my other letters to her.

16

One morning in mid-May, a co-worker came up to me when I swiped my time card to clock in. He broke the news as gently as possible, his voice soft and his eyes concerned over his mask. "Miriam? There was an outbreak at Marina station yesterday. Five carriers tested positive. The rest of their regulars got scared and called in sick—most of their routes are open. The postmaster asked every station to send their most junior carriers. You're going."

I was expendable. My haven was letting me down.

"I heard they sterilized the whole place last night. Sprayed everything, opened all the windows. The Marina PTFs will still be there though. Since you guys don't get any sick days like the rest of us."

He patted me on the back, gave me his phone number in case I needed anything, and went to work. A few other carriers plodded in through the doors, half in surgical masks, half in the white cloth masks they'd given us.

An unfamiliar route with unfamiliar street names. Granted, it was a rich, white, preppy neighborhood on the sunny side of the beach, but given all the overtime mail and my lack of familiarity with the streets, it would take me twice as long to cover. It was good everyone was in quarantine and the station sterilized, but one of their PTFs could have COVID.

Word traveled fast. Another carrier soon approached me: "I heard you're going to Marina. My husband works there. He's home today. Don't worry—Marina's not hard. You'll get a walking route or just drive packages. It's a safe neighborhood."

At my supervisor's desk, I asked Jyothi, "Am I going to Marina?"

She looked me up and down. "Who told you that? I took care of it."

"How?"

"Ayesha will go."

My heart dropped. "But she's more senior than me."

"Let me give you some advice. When someone does something nice for you, say thank you and carry on. But if you're really curious, I told them you were on the verge of quitting yesterday and that I talked you off the ledge. I said transferring you would guarantee your resignation."

"But why Ayesha?"

"I'm trying to get rid of her. I know she has a baby, but she's slow. Hopefully Marina will keep her, and I can apply for a new PTF."

Ayesha followed the rules, listened to the older carriers, and took care of herself—all while pumping milk. Now she was being sent to a station with a COVID outbreak. Meanwhile, I had misdelivered two packages.

"Resy speaks very highly of you," Jyothi continued. "She was the one who talked to your trainer and told me you could case your own mail on the first day. No one has done that before. You

took overtime before most PTFs do, *and* you don't complain."
Jyothi paused, staring hard at me. "Every station is swamped,
and there will be more outbreaks. They're going to ask for you
each time. I'll see how long I can keep you because I know other
stations will try to steal you. Just do me a favor—don't ever bring
back the mail and don't ever get into an accident. I'll look out
for you."

As I walked back to my case, I could see other carriers looking
at me and talking among themselves. One was shaking her head.
Part of me was relieved not to be sent to a COVID station, even
as I felt guilty about Ayesha.

"Teacher's pet," one of the older carriers mumbled as he
walked past me.

I thought of a Korean phrase: *man-gam gyocha*—a four-way
intersection where different emotions crash from every direction.

* * *

The manager's voice crackled over the speaker, and I realized for
the first time that there was a PA in the station. The voice in the
speaker was scratchy and hard to decipher.

One carrier stopped walking with her hamper and said,
"What's he saying? I can't hear nothing over that thing." She
adjusted a package on the verge of falling off. "It doesn't matter.
They only tell us bad things over the PA. It's never 'You're doing
a great job!'" She pushed her hamper out of the building as the
announcement continued, ignoring it completely.

I tried to listen. Something about "Please remember to wash
your hands frequently, social distance, and wear a mask." As I
continued casing my mail, I heard, "And remember, the USPS
cares deeply about our postal employees . . ."

The whole station erupted in laughter. I turned around, amazed to see every one of my co-workers laughing. Some stopped their work to laugh at the ceiling, waving their hands in a gesture of dismissal. One of them shouted at the loudspeaker above, "Then where's our hazard pay?" More laughter. "Why don't *you* deliver these freaking packages?" They might as well have been shouting at God, the way their voices tilted upward. For the first time in weeks, everyone's eyes crinkled above their masks. A darkly wholesome form of fatalism.

*　*　*

"You know how you walk around believing that God loves you?" Esther had once asked. "That's how I feel about our friends."

"But, Esther," I had argued, "all of us will fail you at some point. I won't be there for you one hundred percent of the time, even if I'll try. I think we all need more than our friends, family, whatever."

"It's okay. If you can't be there, someone else will."

We were both wrong. Esther was not there, and neither was God.

"Hi!" It was the retired carrier who lived on my route, calling to me as I sat in my truck drinking water. He had the waddle of a penguin. "I wanted to ask, do you have a uniform?"

"I need to wait. I'm on probation."

"My wife has an unopened one if you want."

"What?"

"One second."

He went into his garage and reached for one of the cardboard boxes that were neatly organized on steel shelves. He opened one of those boxes and procured some shirts in plastic wrapping.

A baby-blue knit shirt with a dark blue collar. Slung over his arm was an old rain jacket that smelled decidedly moldy.

"My wife didn't think her old pants would fit you. These are clerks' shirts because she always liked their uniforms better than ours."

I stared at the uniform in my hands. I had dreamed about this for so long. But this wasn't the shirt I wanted, and I didn't want any more nice gestures or special treatment from anyone at the postal service, even retirees. I was dizzy and wanted to leave. Politely I said, "Thank you. This is very kind of you."

* * *

As I ate my sunflower-seed-butter-and-cherry-jam sandwich for lunch, I checked my phone for news of the outbreak at Marina station. Nothing. It wasn't being publicized. I guessed no one in the Marina would notice that their mail carriers were different today. My desire to pray for Ayesha was blocked up, it had no outlet.

* * *

When I got home, I went to my laptop, looking again for news of the Marina outbreak. My screen glowed in my dark apartment, and Dolmangi curled up by my feet after his last day of barking all day in the backyard. Starting tomorrow he'd go to Patty and Minyoung's. Instead of the Marina, I read about a police officer who killed a man named George Floyd in the streets of Minneapolis. Children were among the witnesses. *Gaeksa*—he died away from home, a stranger, his death a spectacle. Transported to the afternoon I heard of Esther's death—my skeleton ripped out of my body, the elaborate structure of toothpicks (my former life) shattered with cannonballs, the vomit and diarrhea, the recurring image of a knife in my temple. I thought of the people who loved George Floyd. I wondered if they were losing their minds, their hold on their bodies, alienated by their own existence, living a nightmare.

Then there was Floyd himself. No more days to do the things he loved, to grow old and at peace with himself, to say goodbye. I needed to lie down.

When I saw images of the streets filled with protesters, the scale of public mourning, outcry, and resistance, it felt appropriate yet unexpected. Besides occasional uprisings, America's response to daily injustice and loss of human life was so quiet on average. Global quarantine: both an impediment to and galvanizer of mass demonstration. Hordes of people preferred risking infection than suffering privately. Esther's mother's scream pointed to the one in my chest while remaining beyond me. Nothing could prepare me for a sudden death. My life had fallen apart. And yet, some people experienced it continually. Entire communities, young and old, here in the States and abroad, lived with regular, constant death. And I knew now that each loss brought all the other ones back.

> . . . A voice is heard in Ramah, mourning and great weeping, Rachel weeping for her children and refusing to be comforted because they are no more . . .
>> How long, Lord? Will you forget me forever?
>> How long will you hide your face from me?
>> How long must I wrestle with my thoughts
>> and day after day have sorrow in my heart?

I arrived at work the next day bleary-eyed. None of the other mail carriers said anything about George Floyd. I wondered what my co-workers thought about race. My own immigrant parents had occasionally said racist slurs in Korean and had planted small American flags in the flowerpots outside our front doors. Their ideal of a fair America was a narrative they clung to, helping them rationalize leaving everything behind to move here and become subject to countless everyday embarrassments.

I guessed Esther would have been at the protests. She hated racism and the police for all the times they'd barged into her home and did nothing but humiliate her family when the neighbors reported her parents' fights.

I had no chance to deliberate on whether to join in the protests. Delivering mail took up my life.

The picture of Ayesha's baby was no longer up in the case next to mine. Ayesha was in the Marina, where I hoped she was safe from infection. How did it feel for her to hold her baby after George Floyd died? But she had never invited me into her world. She had no reason to. I stopped myself from speculating about her private life.

17

"Miriam!"

The sun wasn't up yet, but it wasn't quite night either. I handed Dolmangi on his leash to Patty, then his food and his water bowl. Minyoung appeared in her pajamas—she'd stayed up to see me. All the humans were masked. Dolmangi, in a great mood after his morning walk, sauntered into their apartment with an open-mouthed smile and his tail waving back and forth. He hadn't smelled or licked another human since the pandemic. It was surreal and painful to be standing in front of Esther's old apartment, but my bitterness had abated. It warmed me to see Patty and Minyoung, and I was confronted by the glow of our old friendship.

"I'm sorry it's so early," I said. "Today's the only day I have Pro Van training. Starting tomorrow, I'll drop him off closer to seven thirty. And I should be back around eight thirty tonight if that's all right."

"That's fine. That sounds like a really long day. Though your uniform looks killer," Patty said.

"Thanks." I posed for them in my clerk's shirt and visor. "How are you doing?"

"We're going crazy," Minyoung said, "like everyone else."

"Are you going to the protests?" I asked.

"We're going to do the caravan from our car," Minyoung answered. "Honking with signs on the Great Highway. It's been closed for pedestrian traffic."

"I see."

"Have you thought of doing anything for Esther's birthday?" Patty asked.

Now this. I'd been avoiding thinking about it. It was approaching in less than a week. I knew it would be a disaster and I wouldn't be okay.

"It would be nice if we did something together," Minyoung said.

"Yeah, let us know if there's an opening in your schedule, even on a weekday. We could do something outside, maybe a picnic," Patty added.

Esther would have been thirty-three. I looked down. "No."

Minyoung and Patty were quiet. Then Minyoung cleared her throat and softly said, "It must be so crazy for you right now."

"I don't want a picnic," I said. "I want to jump in the ocean."

Minyoung quickly responded, "I still have the extra bodysuit she got for me when I went with her."

"Let's do it," Patty said.

We all knew it would be China Beach at dawn, when Esther used to go.

* * *

I arrived at my Pro Van training at seven in a daze. As part of my training, I would be an hour late to the station, but someone else would case my mail and pull it down for me. It was the same driving lot where I had learned to drive the LLV.

I was sitting on the metal folding chair outside the driving instructor's trailer when I saw Ayesha walking toward me, her hair still in the neat bun. One hand gripped a steaming cup of coffee, the other held a small cooler, and a black purse was slung on a shoulder.

"Hi, Ayesha."

"Hey." She sat on the metal folding chair on the other side of the trailer's door.

I didn't know whether I should bring up the guilt I felt over her going to Marina station. I also wanted to show my solidarity with Black people. But everything I thought of saying to her seemed vague and empty. I couldn't avoid the thought that my impulse to speak to her was more about comforting myself than comforting her.

We sat quietly, waiting. I thought of condolences I could offer, comments on the news, none of which sounded right.

"Are you still at the Marina?" I heard myself asking.

"Yeah."

I was relieved she hadn't been moved again. "How is it?"

"It's fine."

"I hear it's only walking with the mail or only driving with the packages. Is that true?"

"Yeah."

"Which one are you doing?"

She looked at me, confused. "Driving."

We were at the Pro Van training. I stared into a crease in my shoe, wanting to hide in it.

"Driving with packages only reminds me of my last job," she said, "when I worked for UPS."

I cautiously looked up at her face. Her eyes looked tired and there was neither kindness nor animosity in them. I was thankful that she spoke to me. "How does it compare? The UPS and postal service?"

"The benefits are better here." After a long silence—"What about you? What'd you do before this?"

"I was a high school teacher."

"Oh. Why'd you become a mail carrier?"

"Because my best friend died." I hadn't said this aloud before.

Above her mask, her furrowed brows released into sympathy. "Was your best friend a mail carrier?"

"No."

"Then . . . ?"

"I lost my faith in God, so I couldn't keep teaching Scripture."

"Wait, what? What does that have to do with the postal service?"

I looked at my hands. My conversation with the old mail carrier came to mind. "I wanted to do something physical. And I wanted to be alone."

She looked at me. "So, you're doing this job to feel better?"

I reddened.

"No, it's cool. Do you, I guess." Ayesha shrugged and glanced down at her watch. The instructor was late.

Then I asked her what I'd asked everyone at church when Esther died: "Have you ever lost anyone before?" I had needed to hear other people's experiences of it.

"Yeah."

I waited.

"My mom's boyfriend OD'd when I was a kid. Not in front of me, but I was in the house when it happened."

"I'm sorry."

"Yeah, well."

Our driving instructor speed-walked toward us trying not to spill the hot contents of his mug. "I'm sorry to keep y'all waiting." He was also Black. I wondered if he had ever experienced traumatic death. I didn't ask.

"The first thing I want you to notice about the Pro Van," the instructor began, "is its height."

* * *

At a stand-up meeting back at the station after my Pro Van training, Jyothi shouted to us, "As you may have heard, due to all the protests and riots downtown, the mayor has set an eight P.M. curfew. It starts tomorrow."

Next to me, a Filipino with gray hair shook his head. "Some of the rioting is getting out of control."

I flinched. Hundreds of years of unpunished murders against a single community, and people worried about department stores? A part of me wanted them to burn everything down.

Jyothi continued, "However, with all the overtime and staff shortages, many of us are rarely done delivering by eight P.M." She waved a stack of papers in her hand. "Carry these letters with you at all times—take them in your postal vehicle *and* your personal vehicles. If you get pulled over by a police officer, it explains your federal exemption from the curfew. You must carry your postal ID with you as well."

> **Law Enforcement Official:** The bearer of this letter with an accompanying U.S. Postal Service identification badge provides essential services of the federal government.

The Postal Service is continuing to fulfill its critical
public service mission by accepting and delivering mail
and packages in accordance with federal law . . .

"Won't they be able to tell by our uniforms?" one carrier
asked.

"I sometimes wear my uniform to go grocery shopping after
work," another carrier added. "They let me cut the line."

"Also!" Jyothi paused for our attention. "There have been
reports of people holding up postal vehicles. One was robbed in
the Mission yesterday." I wondered if it was an armed robbery,
which now worried me. "Remember, if anyone approaches your
vehicle while you're delivering, don't resist. Let them take whatever they want. Your safety is first. I repeat, *do not* try to defend
the mail and packages."

Chuckles and smiles around the circle.

"Take the packages!" one co-worker shouted. "I don't care,
take them all!"

"You know, we really are like little soldiers going out into
war," a young Thai male carrier said to me. He was tall with
glasses.

I laughed.

"No, really! You know our LLV was made by the military,
modeled after military vehicles. We have uniforms, we use military standard time. On all our forms, they call our routes
'tours.'"

He gripped the satchel across his shoulder with conviction.
My smile tapered out.

After the meeting ended and the carriers dispersed, Jyothi
beelined toward me. "Miriam, wait. Listen very carefully. There
was an outbreak in Townsend. They asked for you."

Townsend. Where someone cried every day.

"I tried to do everything to fight for you, but the whole city is shorthanded because of COVID. I'll try my best to get you back soon."

Back soon. Try her best. "Thanks, Jyothi." It was my turn to be screwed over, but at least the blow was softened. I needed to do some penance anyway.

"Hold on, Miriam!" Resy held a large paper grocery bag. She opened it to reveal old uniforms. "Some of the ladies noticed you wearing a clerk's uniform and thought you should have a carrier uniform. These are their old uniforms that are too small for them now, after they had kids. They're all washed and clean, just a little faded."

There were several neatly folded, collared shirts, and stiffly ironed pants. The me who'd longed for these uniforms felt far away. These weren't the items from my wish list, but they were softened by years of wear, personally laundered, and folded by older immigrant women who'd chased away the young men who tried to hit on me. Maybe their old uniforms could act as a protective talisman at Townsend.

"Thank you, Resy. Please tell them thank you."

* * *

The exterior of Townsend station was unassuming, a white building with a small glass door, but inside it was cavernous. They had sixty-six routes compared to Mendell Station's twenty-eight. Most carriers in the station had come from elsewhere. Some of the PTFs were from my training cohort. One looked like a zombie, though his eyes lit up in recognition when I greeted him, only to return to living-dead status when he glanced away. In the vast parking lot, the supervisor held a stand-up meeting to explain where to find the keys, scanners, SPRs, RTS, and hot case. He chain-smoked with his surgical mask on his chin while delivering the announcements. He didn't look concerned about COVID or anything else.

"You drive a Pro Van?" he asked me.

"As of this morning, yes."

"Okay, then take forty-seven." He fished a key out of his pocket.

The shelves in my case were stuffed with letters and flats before I even brought over my yellow tray. Undelivered mail from previous days. Stacks of packages marked *BC*, for "business closed," filled my case as well. Usually the business wasn't actually closed, but it had been too late to deliver. I thought about all the customers on this route, locked in their apartments and waiting through the extreme delays on their mail and packages, and I felt a wave of nausea.

They had two clerks—one just for SPRs and another for large packages—but it seemed they needed three. The stacks of packages piled next to the hampers were taller than the hampers themselves. Unlike our station, there wasn't a muscular carrier to bring the particularly heavy packages directly to one's case. I wrote the order of delivery for the streets on a piece of scrap paper, strategizing how to load the vehicle. An extra ten minutes went to planning, but I needed it. I didn't know the relation of one street to another.

I thought of what a co-worker had told me on Amazon Sunday: "I used to carry my time card in my wallet because every morning they sent me to a different station." I'd been able to keep my time card by the station door the entire time. Carriers in the early aughts went to work at a new station every morning.

I initially enjoyed walking around the back of the Pro Van instead of stooping as I did in the LLV. But when I saw how many more packages the vehicle could hold, I began to retch from anxiety-induced nausea. I told myself to stop being so dramatic. I had chosen the postal service to be alone and do something physical, but this was another level. The day would be long, confusing, and difficult, and I would fail. I felt the futility of organizing packages for delivery only to bring them back. Esther's fatalistic hyena laugh rang in my head, which offered me some comfort. I considered how I would narrate this to her in my letter once I got home, if I didn't collapse into bed first.

There was a solid wall of boxes when I finished loading my Pro Van in the early afternoon. I texted Minyoung and Patty an apology that I would likely return to their place around eight or nine in the evening.

damn that sounds crazy, Patty texted back. *dolmangi can spend the night here. stay safe. <3*

* * *

There were extra barricades and street closures due to the protests and to encourage people in lockdown to take socially distanced walks. I ignored the signs and safety cones, briefly exerting the power of my federal mandate. Broken glass, used masks, and burn marks covered the asphalt.

In a desperate attempt to deliver quickly, I shook or massaged my lighter packages, determining whether they were okay to chuck up the stairs or at the entrances from the sidewalk. Customers might be disturbed to see me hurl their packages at their doors, but it wasn't worse than how the packages were thrown at the station into our hampers and cages. I was *not* working as to the Lord. Resy escorted each package up to the front door, knocked or rang the doorbell, and waited before setting it down gently out of sight. She'd be horrified.

A door-to-door postcard begged people to join the postal service. A cheesy cartoon showed the backside of a superhero in a cape, with a night skyline and speech bubbles announcing a free hiring event at the San Francisco Airport: *The power of your career is in your hands!*

"Be a part of the problem!" one of the carriers had joked at the station, holding up the flyer. Despite my nausea from this morning, the badly pixelated graphic of a Superman cape pulled at my heartstrings. No skilled professional made this. It was made by a graying postal service aunt or uncle at a cubicle using Paint or PowerPoint on an ancient PC. They reminded me of Esther's scrappy punk zines.

Despite the dense urban environment, I felt stranded. My brain focused exclusively on chucking packages and slipping mail. For the first time, I took my full thirty-minute lunch break, during which I ate two cheeseburgers with fries and a large soda. My peanut-butter-and-Concord-grape-jelly sandwich was my late-afternoon snack. After indiscriminate hours of searching for mail openings, walking, throwing, and inserting, sweat dripped down my neck and in my armpits, and my stomach roared again with hunger. Rather than wait to eat at home, I entered a second restaurant for some Vietnamese *bún* with grilled pork and imperial rolls. My legs thrummed with pleasure whenever I sat.

At eight in the evening, I decided to head back. I had four full shelves, five bins, three letter trays, and about five extra-large packages remaining in my vehicle. Instead of feeling dejected, I felt an exhilarated fuck-you satisfaction of making it to the end of the day, pride at being able to pace the empty space of my Pro Van, which had previously been crammed floor to ceiling with mail and packages. I scanned each of my remaining parcels "business closed" and used a Sharpie to write *BC* and the date on the packages themselves. Some of them, I just updated the date on the BC. Squatting and scanning warmed me less than walking and delivering, and the goose bumps on my arms reminded me it was getting cold.

When I went back to the station, the supervisor was still there. Jyothi was never at the station at the end of our day, just the carriers. He sent me right back out. "Finish delivering everything."

I thought of the leftover mail and packages in the case in the morning. The previous carrier hadn't finished the route, why did I have to? "Does everyone else have to finish their entire route?"

"What does it matter to you?" he shouted at me. "When I tell you to finish delivering, you say, 'Yes, sir.' What, you think you're too cute to work? Some of you have been pampered at the other stations."

"I thought you couldn't make us work over twelve hours."

"You're a PTF. It's mandated."

I used the failproof excuse they taught us at training: "I don't feel safe."

"Like I care!"

I hadn't been yelled at since I was a child. I went back to my case to take a breath. An older white carrier with gray stubble and a paunch was putting away his things in the case next to mine.

"Are you finished?" I asked him.

"Finished? I'm regular. I did my time as a PTF. Yo, you gotta go back out?" He talked like a surfer, or punk rocker.

I nodded.

He walked over to my case and scanned the shelves, opened the drawers. He found what he was looking for. A headlamp. He inspected it, pressing all the buttons, handing it back to me with the red light on. "White lights are too bright. There's a flashing light in the back, so people can see you." He rummaged around the case some more, finding a reflective vest and extra batteries. He set them down on the table with a clack. "Dude, how'd you get a uniform as a PTF? I mean it looks used as fuck, but you're hella lucky. People will be less freaked-out when they see you from their windows at night. When I was PTF, I wore street clothes and looked like a creep, 'cause they can't always see your satchel. Also—walk slow. You don't want to fall or trip or nothing or else they'll blame *you* for not wearing the right shoes or some crap. And if customers see you from a distance, they're less likely to get scared and shoot your brains out." He bellowed, "Blast music from your phone or headphones if you have any."

"But at training they said 'I don't feel safe' could get you out of going out late, especially if you've already done twelve hours. Isn't this illegal?"

"I mean, I think they stopped allowing darkness to be a reason to feel unsafe. Alaska and them get dark early in the winter. Plus we're slammed, *plus* you're PTF. But yeah, this technically isn't allowed, but whatchu gonna do about it? I mean, you could lose your job and sue. Have no income for months. Or just deliver the mail and make bank with your V time."

V time was double pay, which kicked in after ten hours. Overtime was one and a half times the pay, which kicked in after eight.

"Ey yo, this is temporary. It gets *much* better once you hit regular."

"Is that after I finish probation?"

He laughed again. "Hell no. It's random. Some PTFs made regular a week after their probation. Me, I waited years. It's based on need. They do it in large batches, like hundreds at a time. So, yeah, depends on your luck."

A lot of the laughter at the postal service was nihilistic.

I drove back to Howard and Ninth, where I had left off. I sat for a while in my driver's seat staring off into the distance. Finally, I donned my headlamp, bathing the inside of my Pro Van in a red light that swung with every movement of my head. Out on the streets, it must've looked as if a disco light flashed from the back of my head. Some soldier I was.

The later it became, the more pronounced the sound of my footsteps. Apartment buildings towered on either side, most of the windows dark. Some storefronts were smashed in and boarded up, and I carefully avoided the broken glass. I alternated between the cool dark and the warm bright of apartment lobbies, nodding to the night-shift security guards, who wore masks and barely looked up from their phones. The sound of my opening and slamming shut the rows of metal reverberated more than ever. At this hour, my echoes were vast.

Besides a glow of moonlight behind the clouds, the sky was sooty and drab. Its flat, faraway pattern filled every space between the edges of buildings, poles, and wires. The sky had the property of a liquid, conforming to the shape of its container. On the sidewalks without streetlights, figures with blankets over their shoulders huddled around makeshift tents. Some would shout at me, I couldn't tell whether happily or angrily. I walked in a large curve around them. The air became damp with cold, a breeze lifted trash into the air, and though delivering at full speed was no longer a priority, I paced and fingered the mail at a steady pace. I was going to return to the station around eleven and go home no matter what, that bastard could scream himself hoarse. Resy said she did fifteen hours in December, and I thought of her delivering packages at three in the morning like a bootleg federal-employee Christmas elf.

* * *

At six A.M., I received an automated call from the postal service to report to Townsend again. At least Patty and Minyoung were walking and feeding Dolmangi.

When I got to the station, a hamper of packages was covered in blood.

"Don't worry. Hazmat has been notified!" the supervisor shouted from his desk.

A different, scruffy, white carrier next to me whispered, "Yeah right. He didn't call shit. Too many forms to fill out."

"But where did the blood come from?" Was it an employee's or an animal's?

The carrier shrugged. "I think they'll just wipe them down with Clorox. By the way"—he looked me up and down—"how old are you?"

The way he asked felt different from that of the guys at Mendell. "Thirty-three." I hoped the number would scare him.

"You look nineteen. My ex is around your age. Also Asian."

I grimaced hard so he could see it. "Where's the other guy that was here yesterday?" I missed the old, friendly surfer.

"He's off today," the creepy guy said. "I'm the T6."

I turned away and started casing my mail.

"Hell no," came an indignant woman's voice as she stood in front of the supervisor who'd sent me back out the previous night.

"When's the last time this route was delivered? Three days? A week?"

"You could walk with six bundles," the supervisor said. I couldn't tell if he was joking. "Keep three bundles in your arms and three in your satchel."

The carrier picked up an enormous bundle of flats, barely held together by rubber bands. "Six of these? For each block? These are just the flats—what about the letters?"

"Back in the day, we delivered mail without all this yapping." She shook her head and walked away. "Nuh-uh. I quit."

All of us watched her walk out the door. When she slammed her satchel into a trash bin outside, we snapped out of our trance and went back to work. I was filled with admiration and envy.

The scruffy carrier next to me sighed. "She should have talked to me first. I'm the union steward here."

This creep? Townsend really was hell.

*   *   *

Loading my truck to the brim this time didn't give me nausea, but I moved slower. Out on the streets, I kept making small mistakes—forgetting my satchel in my truck, bringing up the wrong batch of packages to the staging area, or turning onto the wrong street minutes after I had double-checked. Around lunch, I texted Patty and Minyoung, asking if Dolmangi could spend another night. Delivering mail on empty streets between skyscrapers, I wasn't sure how Esther's death had brought me to this specific point, and whether this was the correct response to her death, to my still being alive.

At ten thirty in the evening, my scanner lit up with a message. Usually, the midday messages were about hydration and social distancing, but this time it said, RIOTERS IN TOWNSEND PARKING LOT. FOR YOUR SAFETY, DO NOT RETURN TO TOWNSEND CARRIER ANNEX. PARK IN THE REI PARKING LOT 840 BRANNAN ST. MANAGER WILL BE THERE WITH DIRECTIONS. RETURN IMMEDIATELY.

My mind went blank. The only things I wanted were to shower and lie down.

The neighborhood was empty enough to drive in the wrong direction on one-way streets. Even so, Townsend was blocked off completely with safety cones. By the light of a lamppost in the REI parking lot, I could see a Latino carrier coming out of his vehicle, his hair plastered to his forehead and the sheen of dried sweat on his cheeks and neck. A cloth mask hung limply from one ear. He walked toward a gray-haired man in a wind-breaker and black pants standing by a sedan with the trunk popped open. The carrier talked with him and threw the scanner in the trunk. He unhooked his keys from his pants. I pulled up and parked beside them.

"What's going on?" I asked.

The gray-haired man showed us a video on his phone. It was hard to see because of the darkness of the footage, but several people in masks, beanies, and baseball hats were swinging aluminum bats full force at the postal vehicles. Rearview mirrors were shattered. The backs of the vehicles were open. Ripped packages lay discarded on the ground.

"Oh God." Those poor, dented vehicles. They were already on their last legs.

"Don't worry." The manager returned his phone to his back pocket. "The police are on their way, and the video will be used as evidence. We'll get these hooligans."

"Are the police really necessary?" I asked. "Doesn't the postal service have its own inspectors?"

"Destroying undelivered mail is a federal crime. You should know that from your training. And don't get me started on all the paperwork I'm going to have to fill out because of this."

I forced my thoughts away from the rioters and the accursed Townsend customers. I didn't feel like breaking down in front of people I didn't know.

"What about our undelivered packages and outgoing mail?" the other carrier asked.

"Leave them locked in your vehicle. The clerks will be here in a few hours and take care of them. Which will, of course, make tomorrow even slower."

"Honestly, if they wanted more stuff, they should have come in the morning, when the vehicles were full," the other carrier said.

The manager rolled his eyes.

I smiled in spite of myself. "What station are you from?" I asked the other carrier.

"Potrero. You?" His hand on the strap of his backpack was covered in tattoos.

"The Outer Richmond."

"I heard about you!" the manager said.

I shriveled.

"I heard you delivered a full route in your first three days. That's really impressive."

I was tired, stressed, and sad, not in the mood. The world was falling apart, Esther was dead, God was no longer there, and Black people were being killed by the police.

"I usually have Wednesdays off," I told the manager. "Does that mean I can stay home tomorrow?"

The manager laughed. "Most of the carriers at this station haven't had a day off in months."

* * *

Back at my apartment, I missed Dolmangi. He was better off sleeping and eating at normal hours indoors with my friends. I wondered if he missed me. I washed off the day, put my wet hair up in a bun, and donned a large T-shirt. I lay corpse-pose on the carpet. I thought about the bloody packages, empty streets with broken glass, and masked people beating up postal vehicles with metal bats. My body was tired, but my mind was spinning at a thousand revolutions per minute. I went to the kitchen.

> Esther. How did I believe in hell for so long? What made me okay with it? I remember thinking people who dismissed it were naïve. Did you ever wonder about my belief in hell? When your favorite aunt died of cancer, you asked what I thought about the afterlife. I said the soul was eternal. I didn't allow myself to think past that for your aunt.
>
> I didn't believe in hell just because my parents taught it to me. The idea of hell always *felt* correct, and I harbored a constant dread that my life was being pulled into it. I saw how people died of starvation while literal tons of food and crops were burned to control prices, how a bottle of wine was worth more than an enslaved child, how plastic and poisons floated in our blood. Every day without pause people did atrocious things.
>
> You agreed that humans sucked, but you left it at that. I was convinced there was a potential for evil within every human but also a darker force of evil outside us and

beyond us. (Now maybe I'd call it history and institutions.) The barbarity of hell in the world to come mirrored the hell in the world as it was. Hell seemed tragic, natural, and inevitable.

To be honest, I never liked the idea of hell. A lot of people do, including oppressed people. You might, too, because of your categorial hatred for unfairness and pretention, including your categorical hatred for Audi drivers or asshole Giants fans who were the reason you tattooed "FTG" (Fuck the Giants) onto your toes. Some people want violent punishment for the genocidal dictators, mass murderers, child traffickers. Before being sent off to death camps in the Holocaust, some Jews asked their surviving family members to avenge their deaths. I remember reading about an enslaved woman before the Civil War who comforted her peers by prophesying that white people's blood would flow like a mighty river. I'm sure some people want hell for dirty cops, repeat offenders . . .

But when I think of hell, all I can think of is my father's bruised and swollen face. My mother's skinny, wasting body. Your corpse on the train tracks. I don't want any violence done to the human form. I want to maintain its integrity—mind and soul.

Even when my mom beat the shit out of my dad, I didn't want her punishment. I wished she would stop. For us to understand each other, feel each other's pain. I pitied her and wanted her love.

Isn't restorative > punitive? Or are you someone who wanted both? The God of the Bible wants both. I regret not asking you about this, though now I remember you singing at the top of your lungs Patti Smith's "Jesus died for somebody's sins but not mine." Was that your opinion of this entire framework?

Hell as a punishment for bad people *isn't even how it works.* Protestants believe ALL humans are evil, worthy of condemnation—even charitable, loving people who don't believe in Jesus go to hell. And a genocidal dictator can avoid hell if they just confess Christ on their deathbeds. How's that for justice?

Are you not allowed in heaven? Are there no drag queens in heaven? Do gays turn straight there? That place sounds awful.

My idea of justice in the afterlife: 1. Every human filled with the knowledge and experience of the suffering they'd caused others. Even if it's excruciating, hell-like, or takes centuries for someone to understand the misery they caused. 2. Every human made to understand everyone who hurt them, even when it was done irrationally.

Everyone would be comforted by each other, by God. Those who were hurt more would be comforted still more. You, your parents, your brothers, your old dispensary crush, George Floyd, every oppressed group—comforted exactly as they needed. The wicked need a type of comforting, too—the amount of loneliness, fear, rage they must have to be able to do what they've done, to face what they've done. But their victims would be comforted more. That's what the resurrection meant to me—life over death, love for our enemies (including when our enemy is ourselves), redemption over condemnation, mercy over justice.

But I can't avoid Bible verses about the "sheep sepa-rated from the goats," "the wheat and the chaff," the binary of those who get God and eternal life, and those who go to "the place of weeping and the gnashing of teeth." You're either in or you're out. Eternal bliss or hell.

Was this why you never accepted Christianity even when you visited my church on Sundays? Did you smell something fishy?

I no longer like how homeless, foot-washing Jesus ends up returning in Revelation with a golden sash, trumpets, monstrous armies, and a sword in his mouth, throwing nonbelievers into a fiery pit—all that Imperial Rome. That wasn't your style either.

If I can't stand a hell based on Christian values, then how can I love a God who did?

I looked at the time. It was past two in the morning. I hadn't stretched and I needed to get up in five hours. The next day was here and assuredly bad. Still, I folded the letter, placed it in an envelope, pressed a stamp down, crossed it out, wrote the addresses and *RTS dec.* I dropped it into my satchel.

Then I saw the date. It was the day before Esther's birthday.

18

The last time I saw Esther alive was mid-January. She came by my apartment to pick up her oversize dark olive jean jacket, which she'd she left at my place while dog-sitting for New Year's. Dolmangi was as excited to see Esther as he was to see me. She let him lick her face, whereas I didn't. She joked that she'd date Dolmangi if he were human, so she could have a handsome jock boyfriend. Her engine was running when I came out in my pajamas and glasses; she was on her way to get groceries. I handed her the jacket, we hugged as usual. She smelled of pheromones, sunblock, and her unique blend of essential oils—cloves, lavender, eucalyptus, geranium, peppermint—a mix she concocted from sales-bin selections from Gross Out. Neither of us knew she would be dead in a week.

The last time I'd spent meaningful time with Esther was before I left for New Year's, the last week of December. We had rented a cabin, her birthday gift to me, even though my birthday was in November. The cabin was an hour and a half from San Francisco, half an hour from Tomales Bay—where Patty, Minyoung, Esther, and I had discount "Shuck Your Own" oysters overlooking the sparkling water for lunch. The cabin had two bunk beds and a heater, with a fire ring and picnic table outside. Patty, Minyoung, and Esther prepared all the food while I played with Dolmangi. Dinner was chili made and frozen in advance, but it didn't thaw in time, so we took turns hacking at it in the jar, emptying frozen chips of chili into the pot as the evening became cold and dark. There was also birthday cake (gingerbread, my favorite), wine, beer, weed, and three bundles of firewood. The next morning there was breakfast (coffee, English muffins, cheesy eggs, avocado, and Cara Cara oranges). Lunch was kimchi fried rice with Spam; dinner was instant ramen. In between cooking and cleaning, we went hiking—up the hill, down to the creek. While we hiked, we rotated conversation partners or spoke to the whole group. I was closest to Esther as Patty was to Minyoung, but I spoke more easily with Patty, and Esther was tighter with Minyoung. We all liked one another. After dinner, they gave me a Clarice Lispector novel with a card they had signed.

* * *

The last time I hung out with Esther one-on-one was dinner at my apartment a week before the cabin trip. She wore a kelly-green bandanna as a scarf around her neck and silver hoop earrings from the craft section of Michaels. Her sunglasses, plastic tortoiseshells from Target, had hair ties looped around the ends because they kept falling off her face. Her flannel jacket was the one she had found on the sidewalk; it was missing a couple buttons. Esther had a way of turning discarded objects into signature items. She painted landscapes and still lifes on the backs of paper grocery bags, on the cardboard side of frozen fish stick boxes. On the backs of receipts or napkins at restaurants, she wrote playlists for different moods and occasions, e.g., "Moving to New York" or "Beer for Breakfast."

I'd recently encouraged her to go to my hairdresser, who was expensive but talented. About the softly angled layers and bangs that framed her face, Esther had said, "It feels like I'm wearing a fashion statement on my head." Then she'd doused her hair with Sun In, turning it brassy. "Did I go overboard?" she'd asked.

"Are your neighbors home?" she said as we walked to my front door.

"Not yet." She took off her shoes, carried them in one hand, put on house slippers.

Dolmangi followed us into the kitchen. Esther set down the bottle of wine she'd brought, took off the house slippers, put on her own shoes, and went out the back door from my kitchen. She left the door open and Dolmangi rushed out to play. She threw him a ball and lit a cigarette. She wouldn't smoke if my neighbors were home, on account of their two school-age children.

I talked to her through the open door as I dressed the cucumbers. "Was Garret there today?"

"Fuck my life, yes." Her laugher was loud, self-deprecating, and nervous. Garret was a paraprofessional who worked with students with moderate-to-severe disabilities. Esther subbed at the school often enough to build a rapport with him but irregularly enough to keep it thrilling. She fell in love with him when one of the students asked if he could smell Garret's hair. Garret took off his beanie and obliged, smiling and closing his eyes while the student deeply inhaled. He was also hot, Esther added. Her last romance had been several years before at the hostel in Nashville, though lately she'd been having more frequent crushes around the neighborhood and at work. Garret was her number one. She thought she saw him everywhere. No matter what part of town we were in—the Richmond, the Mission, or downtown—Esther would duck or look behind her and say, "Oh my God, is that him?"

I hadn't touched or felt attracted to anyone since my suicidal days. Giving up masturbating quieted my sexual desires significantly. I guessed it had transmuted into spiritual desires, or some hungry way of looking at the world. I couldn't picture myself having sex again, and a part of me was sad I'd never experience it while sober or in love. But we couldn't all have everything.

While we were eating, Esther asked for a piece of paper. Then she diagrammed the classroom, indicating the setup of the tables, the location of the chairs and door. Then she indicated where she was sitting, where Garret was sitting, and where other kids and paras were sitting during the movie. Arrows showed how they moved around the room when it was time to put up the chairs. Then she got up from her side of the table and came close to me, demonstrating the proximity with which Garret sat or stood next to her.

"So, what do you think?" she asked.

"I think he's into you!" I meant it. "I think you should ask him to grab coffee or something. Be really chill about it."

"I don't know. I don't like talking to him in front of the other paras. Like they're all watching, and it's like some show." Her upper lip rose in disgust.

"Yeah, and they're always around." I had subbed in those moderate-to-severe disabilities classes before.

After dinner, we went for our usual walk to the beach, meandering up and down rows of tightly packed pastel-colored houses on the way, the ocean breeze blowing our hair into our faces. Dolmangi was ecstatic that Esther's visits meant an extra walk. I didn't remember what we talked about that evening.

I associated our conversations with the practice of beating a rug until no dust was left on it. We emptied out every thought and feeling we had in our minds. There was nothing memorable about it.

* * *

That night, I dreamed Esther came over to my apartment, visibly in pain. I was overjoyed she was back from the dead but concerned because she kept wincing. Then she showed me the long line of stitches along the sides of her body, and the enormous tumor on the back of her neck. When I awoke, I wondered if my attempts to remember her were a rough stitching-back-together that would never match the vibrant person she was while alive. Soon, she would fade away. I would remember less and less. The intense pain and yearning would eventually diminish. A relief I wouldn't know how to hold.

19

I woke up to a call that I could return to Mendell Station. I almost cried in relief yet thought of those still stuck at Townsend. Was it luck or God's unevenly distributed love? (If He existed.)

A few carriers at Mendell Station gathered around my case. "Is it true Townsend was attacked by rioters last night?"

"They just beat up some vehicles in the parking lot." I yawned, and they went back to their work.

Without registering anything, I loaded my packages. Pulled down my case. Drove out to my route. My mental state reminded me of the video from training: "Do you ever arrive at your destination and wonder, 'How did I get here?'"

I was in the middle of a U-turn when a truck behind me was suddenly too close; then it zoomed up against my left window. I slammed on my brakes but still skimmed the side of the truck, bending the step to its side door.

I pulled over. Power tools and a ladder were on the bed of the truck, and the driver, a fit, middle-aged Asian man, was deeply tan and wrinkled.

"I'm sorry," I sputtered, on the defensive. U-turns were illegal in an LLV because with the driver's seat on the right, the left-side blind spot was enormous. The only way to see behind us was with a series of five rearview mirrors, but we all made illegal U-turns.

He walked over to the side of his truck, running his fingers along the dent. He tried pushing it back in place. "I'm going to need to take this in."

I wiped my sweaty palms on my shirt. "I'm so sorry."

He rubbed his forehead. "Are you going to get in trouble for this?"

"One second, can I make a call?" I stepped around the corner and called Resy, explaining the situation.

To my surprise, Resy didn't yell or sigh in disappointment. "It's okay. Accidents happen. Text Jyothi. Meanwhile, take a picture of his driver's license and your driver's license, of his car and your car. Get his phone number. Don't give him yours."

I did as I was told, and the man drove off. Then Jyothi texted back.

What's your cross street? Stay where you are. I'll be there in about twenty minutes.

After the obligatory pictures, I was alone on an empty street. My vehicle stood still, holding most of the day's mail and packages. My arms were empty, so I hugged myself and paced, unsure what would happen next. Would I have to pay for the repairs? Would they suspend me without pay or send me back to Townsend? Was Resy gentle with me because my head was about to go on the chopping block?

Then, on the corner, I recognized the Mr. Burns posture of a mail carrier—skinny and hunched over as he slipped mail into a house.

"Manwai!"

He looked up. I ran over to him. "I got into an accident," I told him, my mouth dry. I knew he had a screw-everyone attitude, but I wanted consolation, pity, advice, anything. I pointed at the intersection. "Right there."

"Are you okay?" he asked calmly.

I nodded.

"Did anyone get hurt?"

I shook my head. "The other guy's step on his truck was a bit dented."

"Not too bad. Did you apologize?"

"Yes."

He shook his head. "The minute you say sorry, it's game over. You could have blamed the shoddy brakes. With these crappy old vehicles, no one would have been able to argue."

I tried to remember if the brakes were indeed slow. "But I was making an illegal U-turn."

"How far into the turn were you?"

"Just started."

"For all anyone knows, you were making a left turn, period. Anyways, next time, don't apologize."

I hoped there wouldn't be a next time. "Have you ever gotten into an accident while delivering?"

His eyes widened as if accused. Then he took a deep breath. "Yeah. My first month on the job."

"What happened?"

He looked me in the eye. "I got fired."

"Oh my God." Then I noted his uniform, the mail in his hands.

"They hired me back. They needed people," he said flatly in his baritone. "Don't worry about it. You'll be fine."

"I won't get in trouble? And will I have to pay for the other guy's repairs?"

"No, the postal service has its own auto insurance. I doubt you'll get in trouble. We're shorthanded as hell. Hey, it's okay." It was the most kindness I had ever received from Manwai. He actually seemed sympathetic.

A Hyundai pulled up behind my vehicle. Jyothi stepped out. I turned back to Manwai. "Sorry to keep you from your work."

"No worries. I have all day."

"And thanks for your words. I feel a bit better."

I jogged over to Jyothi, who was walking around and inspecting my vehicle. I was confused why our clerk was also sitting in her car.

Without a hello, Jyothi said, "I'm supposed to get someone else to deliver your mail and suspend you from driving for a week, but we both know there's no time for that. So, this accident happened after you finished delivering all your mail, okay?"

"Okay." This seemed easy to disprove, but I trusted Jyothi to know what we could get away with.

"When you get back to the station, write down what happened, sign and date it, and leave it on my desk."

"I can't deliver mail for a week?"

"You'll deliver mail with Nico. In a two-ton."

"What about his mail?"

"You'll deliver both routes together. He'll do all the driving." Then she said something surprising. "Now let's reenact the accident. You need to hold my phone and record a video while I drive your vehicle. Tuan will drive my car and pretend to be the truck behind you."

"What? Why?"

"I need to give a PowerPoint presentation to the managers and HR and include a video reenactment. Standard procedure and a solid pain in the ass. So, tell me what happened."

The postal service never ceased to amaze me. How did it manage to be so tedious and boring yet loopy and absurd? Before we started shooting, I used my hands to demonstrate what had happened—my right hand was my vehicle, the left hand was the truck. Jyothi and Tuan focused intently, then asked questions.

"Did he fully stop at the stop sign after you started moving?" Tuan asked for her role as truck driver.

"My guess is barely."

"Good thing it's a cloudy day," Jyothi said. "Soft light is the best."

I directed the short film of my own accident, with my boss in the mail truck and the clerk in a personal vehicle as actors. After the first take, we gathered around Jyothi's phone and watched the recording. I told them what they needed to improve. I ordered Jyothi to turn slightly to the right before turning left. I instructed Tuan to tailgate a little harder. They tried again, both stopping before impact as they did the first time. The third try was perfect. *Cut!* I thought in my head. There was too much meaning to process, or none at all.

"You missed your day off, didn't you?" Jyothi asked after we finished filming. "Take tomorrow. I can tell you need some rest. Wendy will be in because she switched with Mark."

* * *

I continued delivering the rest of the day's mail with a weight tied to my heart. I was both relieved and ashamed to no longer be a precocious delivering savant. And tomorrow was Esther's birthday. *I can finally pick Dolmangi up today. Thanks so much for watching him so much on short notice. China Beach tomorrow at 5:30am?* I texted Patty and Minyoung. All my movements felt slow. A mail truck slowly drove by me and stopped. It was Manwai. He rolled down his window.

"How did it go?"

Used to delivering my mail without any co-workers seeing me, I felt exposed, with my strategies and habits on display—how I left the postal key box open while I propped open the gate with my foot and stretched my body to insert the mail within.

"I made a movie of my accident, and I can't drive for a week. Nico will drive us around in a two-ton."

"Not bad."

"Are you done delivering?"

"Pretty much." He parked and stepped out. "Here, why don't we split the rest of the block?" He took half of my letters and flats. I was quieted by his charity.

We met back at the vehicles. "This is how it'll be when you deliver with Nico," Manwai said. "You'll split the blocks with him."

I nodded. Esther would have liked Manwai. He didn't sugar-coat anything, didn't need to befriend everyone, but he was sympathetic to the downcast. Esther would have worked harder than Manwai, but who knows, maybe if she lived as long as he did, she, too, would deliver with deliberate slowness in order to trade plant cuttings with her customers and save her joints for playing tennis with friends. I took out all of Esther's letters from the front pocket of my satchel and handed them to Manwai.

He read the faces of each envelope, one after another. "Who's Esther?"

I flinched at his voice saying her name. "My best friend."

He saw the abbreviation for deceased. "When did she die?"

"January."

"I'm sorry for your loss."

"Thank you." Even though it had been almost six months since her death, even in sixty years, I thought, this would be the right response, because a loss didn't happen just once; every day afterward was a day the lost ones weren't there.

"Did you send these? The stamps are crossed out, but the return address is . . ."

"No. I pretended." My childhood apartment didn't exist anymore. After it was condemned, nothing was built in its place.

"My sister and father died the year I was supposed to become a postal inspector." He took off his hat. His wispy white hairs stood up.

"I'm sorry for your loss."

"Thanks."

"How did they die?"

"My sister died of lupus. My dad died of cancer."

We stood in silence.

"I was really close to my sister," he said. "That was a bad year."

I imagined a younger version of him with black hair, delivering mail with double grief in his chest. He handed me back my letters.

"I don't know what to do with them," I said.

"You could drop them off in the RTS bins. It would probably be sent to the dead letter office in Atlanta."

I remembered it from the handbook. Where undeliverable, unreturnable mail was kept. "And then?"

"It could get sold at an auction. The buyer wouldn't be able to open it until after they bought it."

That sounded like something Esther would have liked. Letters from her best friend mixed in with a bunch of thwarted pleas and rants. But I needed a witness. I extended the stack of letters to Manwai once more. "Could you please do it for me?"

He accepted them into his hands, and I was filled with an inexplicable relief when I saw him tuck the letters into the front pocket of his satchel. "I'll take care of it."

He put his hat back on and waved goodbye. I watched his vehicle pull away and head back to the station.

20

Happy birthday, Esther.

It was my first thought when I opened my eyes before my alarm went off. At first, I didn't know where I was, but I remembered I spent the night at Patty and Minyoung's in your old apartment. Dolmangi and I slept in your old room with the windows open, while Minyoung slept in Patty's room. The altar would be handsome enough to entice you to visit. We had a COVID-safe slumber party for your birthday.

I couldn't stop crying when I woke up. I felt the same degree of pain when you first died. I can't put into words how fucked up it is that you're not here to get older. It helped that we had to get ready to go to the beach. Minyoung lent me her swimsuit, and we were sniffling in our masks in the car to China Beach with the windows down and our hair flying everywhere.

You were scared of therapy, that you would be diagnosed with something awful and uncurable. You said your therapy was dipping in the ocean. You went at dawn, even in the winter. It's true you made more collages, paintings, clay objects, and piñatas after you started swimming. You started looking into grad schools, even asking if you could come to church with me. You asked everyone there the same question: Do you ever doubt all of this?

I never went swimming with you like you asked. I was waiting for spring, for it to get warmer. Surfers were the only others crazy enough to go into the water in the winter at dawn, and they wore wet suits. I'm sorry I never went with you while you were alive. You mostly wore the beige one-piece you got during your Lands' End phase, when you kept asking me if I wanted anything so we could combine our orders and get free shipping. The straps were too long so you tied large knots at the top of your shoulders. You wore sweat shorts to cover your pubes that stuck out.

In the ocean, every fiber in me shrank—the pores of my scalp, the beds of my fingernails, even my coochie clamped up. The waves pushed my breath out in irregular rhythms. When it got tolerable, I started to swim— another level of shock. I could hear Patty and Minyoung gasping—Minyoung even shouted out curses and laughed. The slick, icy currents rocked against me, and my buoyed limbs clawed and kicked in the frigid darkness, every inhale slipping salt into my mouth. I thought of how your crowded teeth would have glowed from your smiling in the dark. At times, it felt like I was sharing the morning with you, and then your absence would suffocate me. Like I was making a new memory with you, while you appeared and disappeared beside me.

After our flailing about, the sun began to rise. We left the water, one at a time, and my teeth chattered violently. The receding currents sucked water out from under my toes, and the breeze accosted me. I sat on my towel, in my jacket. Minyoung said you were psycho for doing this several times a week. Patty said she never felt so alive, so clearheaded. I agreed with them both. Then we got quiet because every state of matter—liquid, gas, solid—ocean, sky, sand—shifted into different colors: cantaloupe, rose, lavender, peri-winkle, hazel, ash, and sage—until finally the sky stayed azure, the ocean deep navy, and the sand a metallic light brown, all with mischievous stillness, as if nothing had happened.

I called your parents and texted your brothers. Your mom said she was lucky to be your parent, and that you were always like friends with each other. Your dad alternately bitched about your cheapness and slovenly life-style, which kind of pissed me off, but he's also heartbroken and lashing out. In a group chat, your brothers sent pictures of you as a child, as a teen, a college student, a young woman. Your oldest brother also sent me a picture of his daughter, your niece. You would have been such a perfect aunt. You would have enjoyed it so much. I'm sad your niece doesn't get to have that, but I'm sure all of us will tell her stories about you, so she knows who you were. If you're a ghost, maybe you can show her some dope, supernatural shit.

You lived thirty-two years. Today was the day you arrived. Your existence was marvelous and unparalleled. A volatile change of colors between the long night and the long day. Your love was worth far more than the pain of losing you—which is a lot.

*   *   *

This letter I didn't put in an envelope with a stamp and an address. I kept it in my satchel, bare and exposed. It wouldn't go anywhere, only wear out a bit around the edges.

21

Back at Mendell Station, word had gotten around that I no longer had route ten. Another carrier had bid on it. I was assigned to the worst route in the station, route thirty-six. Before, it was broken up every day because no regular carrier wanted it. Now, I would be on it until I turned regular. I wondered if this was payback for getting into the accident. I was just happy to be out of Townsend.

A young Greek carrier at Mendell said to me, "I kind of miss the drama of Townsend. I was there when I first started. Every day was an adventure."

Resy came by my new case. "I used to be a T6 for this route. I liked delivering to the museum. The road there is pretty."

"Do you think Jyothi's mad at me?" I asked.

"Nah. Accidents happen in those LLVs. You do everything fast—even getting into an accident!" Her chipmunk laugh. "It's good to be back here, isn't it? Just in time for Dog-Bite Awareness Day. We get free hot dogs." Sure enough, the air smelled like barbecue. Over the loudspeaker, a voice said, "Take a bite out of a dog, and don't let a dog take a bite out of you."

Later that afternoon, several carriers—an older grandma, a big Samoan, Resy, Manwai—arrived one by one, an hour or two apart, like knights on horseback. They came to take some of my packages. They got no overtime for helping me deliver. They knew my first day on the new route would be the hardest, and they showed me compassion.

*   *   *

It was getting dark when a light rain started. I went back to my truck and put on the moldy raincoat I'd been given. I felt a small thrill and imagined my co-workers rolling their eyes at me for it. My first time delivering in the rain. I imagined Ayesha, Resy, Manwai, and the rest of my co-workers out on their routes alone, getting wet, too, as they ambled along sidewalks, front lawns, and stairs to front doors. Endearment extended from my heart out to them, wherever they were. It was probably a familiar nuisance to them now.

The streets looked emptier than ever, and the quiet was punctuated by the occasional whoosh of a distant car. The hood of my raincoat swished by my ears, and raindrops lightly tapped on my head, my shoulders, my chest. Before I knew it, the world transformed. Every color darkened and intensified; slick surfaces gleamed coolly. The lid to the world opened, and a fresh chill descended. Cold, wet pieces of sky fell from thousands of feet above and stained my jacket sleeves, gloves, and pants. I could neither escape it nor retreat indoors. I needed to finish my route. There was giddiness in surrender.

Each magazine and the letter dampened until I pushed it into a mail slot, and then the next magazine and letter were exposed. None of the mail was drenched, but all of it was wet on top and around the ends. When I was only a customer, I retrieved wet letters and ads on rainy days without getting upset about it. Today, the mail would be mussed, slightly damaged, and no one would blame me; no one would think of me.

I was careful not to slip. My body's stiffness and the increasing heaviness of my clothes pushed against the vigor of my muscles. My cheeks and breath emanated heat.

Then I remembered Esther's body was ashes in a box.

Being alive was almost more than I could bear.

Whether or not anyone or anything was there to see me, my spiritual anchors were replaced by every sensation of my body, flooded with the remarkable act of delivering mail in the rain.

I was born again, again, again.

ACKNOWLEDGMENTS

To Amber Oliver, my brilliant champion and editor, and my dedicated team at Bloomsbury: Ragav Maripudi, Katie Vaughn, and Marie Coolman,

Jin Auh, the agent of my dreams, Abram Scharf, and my supportive team at Wylie,

my insightful teachers at UF: David Leavitt, Camille Bordas, Uwem Akpan, and Michael Hofmann,

my dear cohort: Jake Bartman, Molly Gardener, Vix Gutierrez, Ara Hagopian, and Payal Nagpal,

the warm and generous mail carriers at Mendell Station, Zone 21,

Piece and Miya, Janet and Jasper,

and Danny,

thank you for making this book possible.

A NOTE ON THE AUTHOR

J. B. Hwang received her MFA in fiction from the University of Florida. She lived in San Francisco for eight years and worked as a mail carrier during the pandemic. She currently lives in Philadelphia.